A FAE TALE

What Reviewers Say About Genevieve McCluer's Work

Olivia

"There's a playfulness at times, but then the seriousness of the situation hits the reader square in the face. At the halfway mark it suddenly took off for me. There was one heck of a surprise, that I did not see coming at all. I enjoyed the story and would like to read more in this world."—*Kitty Kat's Book Blog*

Thor: Daughter of Asgard

"Norse mythology intrudes on a bubbly romance in this light adventure from McCluer. ...Readers will come for the gender bending mythology and stay for the light romance."—*Publishers Weekly*

My Date With a Wendigo

"*My Date with a Wendigo* is a sweet, second chance romance at its furry little heart."—*Wicked Cool Flight*

By the Author

My Date with a Wendigo

Olivia

Thor: Daughter of Asgard

A Fae Tale

A Fae Tale

by

Genevieve McCluer

2021

CREDITS
EDITOR: BARBARA ANN WRIGHT
PRODUCTION DESIGN: SUSAN RAMUNDO
COVER DESIGN BY TAMMY SEIDICK

Acknowledgments

Thank you to Jessica, Danny, Alexandra, and Kas for all of your support and help, and to my editor, Barbara.

Prologue

It happened fifteen years ago, back in the old country, when I was six. Mama had told me not to wander off, but I got bored when she was hanging the clothes out to dry. The woods by our house were neither large nor dangerous, and I thought if I found a mushroom or two, then she'd never stay mad.

So I embarked on my quest. I don't recall if I was a princess or a witch, only that I had to go into the woods. It was all a game. I'd fight some monster, find the mushrooms or save my kingdom— maybe it was both—and then I'd be home before she even had time to worry.

Then I got lost.

Then I found monsters.

I'd expected to slay a dragon or maybe vanquish a troll. I'd picked up a stick along the path, and when I wasn't walking with it, it was my weapon. I found those mushrooms and not in any circle. This isn't some Scottish fable, and the only rings we have are in the grass. But when I turned around, I didn't know where I was.

The woods were small, and the sun was still up, but I was even smaller and had taken a few too many turns. I called for help, and someone answered.

It wasn't Mama, and Papa wasn't due home for hours. I heard a woman's voice, and it was beautiful. I ran for it, skirting around a towering oak, and I heard it again. It seemed someone had come to my rescue.

Except when I found them, they weren't human. My college guidance counselor—my old roommate ratted me out—insisted that I wasn't remembering correctly. Or that I was making it up. It's why I don't tend to tell people about it. Canadians never understand.

My grandma had told me stories about laumes. How they would look after babies or eat them and how they could see the future. It seemed each telling changed their appearance. Sometimes they were beautiful women. In others, they had the bodies of dogs or mares. My favorite version was when they had the talons of a bird and the body of a goat, as she always used that interpretation of them for when they ate the baby. It must've been her Catholic upbringing.

What I saw was all of that. One woman had talons and the legs of a goat; another had the body of mare. They were all wearing simple white linen dresses, so I can't say what else looked inhuman. The third, however, looked nearly like a normal girl. She was almost my size and had hair and skin even fairer than mine, though she only had a single eye.

The child stared at me, and I stared back. Sometimes, I wonder why I didn't try to raise my walking stick. It was meant for battling monsters, after all.

Rather than eating me, the two grownup laumes beckoned me forth, and in a singsong voice, with breath that smelled of an early morning rain—I always remember that part—one called out, "Come here, child." Though, of course, in Lithuanian.

Now from what I've heard, you all had "stranger danger" and the like. We were taught to actually be polite, so I went toward her, staring at the imposing being, her goat legs making her look shorter than her body seemed to demand. Despite this, she was still an imposing presence, but her serene face provided comfort rather than fear. "What is your name, child?"

I swallowed. "Dovana, ma'am."

"And I'm sure you are." I'd been hearing the same joke all my life. It was almost reassuring in this context. I am my parent's "Gift." "My name is Matina, and this is Julija." She gestured to the laume with the mare's body.

The young one ran up to me, extending her hand. "And I'm Roze. I've never met anyone who looked weird. What are you?"

"Child," Matina said.

"But she's weird!"

"I don't look that different from you," I protested. How could she be the one saying I looked weird? They were monsters!

"Yeah, you do." Her eye widened, then narrowed, and she peered closer, leaning in to study me. "Weird."

I looked to make sure she didn't have bird feet or anything.

"What are you?" she repeated.

Matina answered for me. "She's a human, dear."

Roze stared, her jaw dropping. Then, to my great surprise, rather than trying to eat me, she hid behind a tree.

The older monster chuckled, waving off the excitable little girl-creature. "Don't worry about her. She means no offense."

I studied the tree, her hand barely poking past it as she cowered. I couldn't imagine why she'd be scared of me. I was only a human, a child. I'd barely even seen past the outer reaches of Babtai, except for a few trips to Vilnius with my papa. How could I have posed the slightest threat to a laume? "Why is she scared of me?"

That laugh will stick with me, I think, until the day I die. There was the sound of thunder in it, but only the comforting elements, not the worry of being struck by lightning or even the frightening bang. "She's never seen any of your kind before, child, and there are many tales of the horrors you wreak."

"Yeah, well, I could say the same." Let's pretend I didn't stick my tongue out at a child-eating monster.

A strangely human hand rested on my head. Here it was; she was going to eat me. I closed my eyes, ready to face my doom. "What has brought you here, child? This is no place for you."

"I live here," I insisted. At the time, it seemed if I confessed that I was lost, she'd see all the more reason to eat me.

Her smile was perfect. Serene. Lovely. Teeth flashed, and they weren't the wicked fangs I'd expected but instead a pleasant warm grin with the slightest overbite. "You must be the newest addition to that family. We've seen them before, out harvesting...well..." She gestured at the pocket I'd stuffed the mushrooms in. "Why don't you run home? I'm sure they're very worried."

I stared at her, barely willing to blink. I had no choice. "I…" It didn't want to come out.

"Do you not know the way? Oh, sweet child." Sweet? I took a step back. "We can guide you back." Her goat legs took a step back, her talons digging into the soft dirt as she pivoted, looking to the tree Roze had hidden behind. "Perhaps my daughter could guide you. She needs to overcome her fear."

At least she'd have more trouble eating me. And I still had my stick. "Okay," I squeaked, the fear taking my voice.

"Roze," she called.

"No!"

"Roze," she repeated.

Several seconds passed. When it seemed that she was intent on ignoring her mother, Roze finally stomped out from around the tree, looking anywhere but me. "I don't wanna. What if she…" Her gaze fell on me for the barest instant, but she never finished the thought.

"Child. Take her home."

"But…" Another stomp and she peeked around her mother to me, doing her best to keep her distance. "You live at that house on the western edge of the woods?"

I nodded.

"Fine." With a leap to the side, as if to keep well out of my reach, she gestured for me to follow her and led me away from the safety or danger of the older laumes. It was a relief. I think. At least I was headed home.

We walked in silence for what felt like hours, but given that I was a child and brushing my teeth felt like hours, I assume it was less. The sun was still well above the horizon when I glimpsed it through the trees.

"Why do you hate humans?" I asked when I could hold it in no longer. "What have we ever done?"

She glared at me and rolled her eye, turning her gaze back to the forest floor and the roots jutting out before us. "Like you don't know. Mother read me the stories. I know what humans do. Your kind lives to kill us. You hunt monsters. You slay dragons. You butcher trolls. Why would I ever trust you? I don't know why they want me to help you, but if they didn't..." She huffed and stomped her foot. "Well, I'd do something awful."

Even at the time, the irony wasn't lost on me. I'd set out that very day with dreams of fighting dragons and trolls. But not real ones. I wasn't actually a murderer. I wasn't the monster she made me out to be, no human was. "That's not true," I insisted, ignoring my cognitive dissonance. "You're the ones who hurt people. Mama has told me the tales. She told me about how you eat babies and toss their bodies at their mother's feet. You're bad." The words sounded more certain than I felt. After all, they hadn't eaten me, had they?

She wheeled on me, coming the closest she'd ever been, staring right into my eyes. Well, one of them. "We would never. I would never. You're the bad guys."

"Nuh-uh!"

"Yuh-huh!"

It went on like that for a while.

She groaned. "Well, then, what were you doing here?"

"I was looking for mushrooms." I could have told her that I was playing, but then she'd have asked what I was playing, and that would take us back into the argument.

"Prove it."

I pulled a mushroom from my pocket.

She studied it for a moment, and her features relaxed, her glare diminished, and she granted me a smile, one like her mother's but with a missing tooth. "Oh, why didn't you say so?"

"Do you want one?"

She shook her head. "I don't like mushrooms. I like bread."

I hadn't picked any bread in the woods, so I offered an, "I'm sorry."

"It's okay." She shrugged, looking at the mushroom and then the trail ahead. "It's a long walk still." The woods were maybe a square kilometer, and we must've already walked at least that distance in a straight line. "Want to play?"

Of course I did. So we played. She picked up her own stick and fought me, and then we fought evil humans coming to kill the monsters. It was her idea. When we finally made it home, the sun was touching the western horizon, and we were both exhausted.

"That was fun," Roze said.

"Yeah!"

We ran up to the door, and Mama opened it, looking terrified. "Vana! I've been worried sick." She pulled me into her arms, squeezing the air out of my lungs. "Where did you run off to? We've looked everywhere. Your papa is still out with the neighbors looking for you, but I thought you might…did you smell dinner cooking and come home?"

I shook my head, but I'm not sure that she noticed.

"What happened? I told you to stay right there. Where did you…Vana, you can't run off like this."

"I know, Mama. I'm sorry. I was out playing with my new friend." I gestured back, and she finally released me. "Can she stay for dinner?"

"What friend?"

I turned around, looking every which way, but Roze was simply gone. The stick she'd been playing with lay in the dirt as the only sign that she was even real. "She was right there." I pointed hard enough that it seemed it would will her back.

"Well, perhaps she'll come back later," Mama said.

With another glance into the woods, I nodded. Maybe she wasn't hungry. "I found some mushrooms."

"That's great, dear. Go inside and set the table. I'm going to try to let your father know to come home."

She found him quickly, I explained what happened, and we had a normal family meal, though I was not allowed dessert. Since I couldn't have it, I asked Mama to leave it out for Roze in case she came back after I went to bed. It had been a long day, and I was very tired.

In the morning, the cookies were gone, replaced with two gold bars. That convinced my parents that the story was true. They celebrated and started making plans to move. They considered Vilnius, then America, but only years later did we ever end up in Toronto.

I haven't seen Roze since. I do get letters, though.

CHAPTER ONE

DOVANA

It's 2009, in Toronto, Canada, and a loud blaring sound keeps erupting from the other side of the room. It grows muffled and finally stops. Not wanting to let any light in, I keep my eyes shut and turn onto my side, facing the wall and trying to will myself back to sleep.

Just when I start to drift back into my dreams, the blaring starts up again, screaming like a klaxon. The noise stops and is followed by the sound of something hitting the wall and feet hitting the ground. "Gah!" my roommate roars. Caroline normally snoozes her alarm at least three times. If she keeps doing like today and only snoozing it once, I'll be grateful. Now I can finally sleep.

"Do you know where I put my *Foundations of Econometrics* textbook?" she asks. "It's not in my bag, and I can't find it."

My silence doesn't seem to satisfy her, as she doesn't start moving again. I can hear her breathing behind me. "I'm asleep."

"But have you seen it?"

Groaning, I roll over, swinging my feet off the bed. "I think it was on the microwave."

Her wide lips split into a grin, and if I wasn't exhausted, I'd find it hard to be mad at her. Brown eyes crinkle, and her ponytail sways as she sprints the few feet to our microwave. The kitchen is in the bedroom, as is every other room save the bathroom. "Yep. It's here. Thank you."

I mutter a response in Lithuanian and lay my head back on my pillow. I don't have to be up for two more hours, as I was not mad enough to sign up for a seven a.m. class.

The door opens, and I think I'm finally going to be allowed to go back to my dreams when she calls, "Hey, could you grab some toilet paper? I'm gonna be in class all day."

"I'm going to my parent's tonight."

"Steal some from them?" I can hear the awkward smile in her voice.

I sigh. "If you'll let me sleep, then fine."

"You're the best." The door slams behind her, and I'm back in Babtai.

I tap my pen on the table, propping my head up on my other arm. My stomach growls. I'd only had a bagel and coffee for lunch in between classes. Maybe I'll be lucky and Mama will already have dinner ready when class gets out.

"So unlike Aristotle, the existentialists like Simone de Beauvoir and her husband—"

"Jean-Paul Sartre," a student says.

"Yes, I know." Professor Marion rolls her eyes. It isn't even the first time a student has called her out on this habit. She'd explained that it was to challenge norms and give de Beauvoir the credit she deserved. To me, it always comes off as excessive, but I didn't have to go through decades in the field, or maybe de Beauvoir's treatment would've grated on me too. Professor Marion breaks into an explanation on the reading that we should have done, explaining de Beauvoir's theories on sexuality and how Jean-Paul Sartre had ridden her coattails.

As I did the reading and paid attention the last time she went into this rant, I take the time to start the chapter for Friday.

"So they were really okay with dating other people?" a voice asks. Normally, I wouldn't care, but the timid tones of the only other lesbian in the class—we went around to volunteer that information—draws my attention. She's so pitiful, it's hard not to worry about her. She seems to shrink as the entire class looks at her.

"That's not really relevant, Ms. Lester, but from what I've read, more than you'd think, less than they acted like. Now, can we please move to the topic."

"Right, sorry," Abigail Lester squeaks. If she wasn't a freshman, I'd call her cute.

Professor Marion resumes her lecture, speeding through the slides, and doesn't even finish the presentation by the time the bell rings.

It's 4:30, and my father doesn't get off work until five, so I decide to go bother an old friend of mine.

Taya Vasilev started school here the same time as I did—we actually met at orientation—and she was the only student there who wasn't born within a hundred miles of Toronto. At least, judging by accents, I suppose a few could've assimilated better.

We formed a fast friendship, and it turned to more. My parents couldn't have been happier when I broke up with her. They'd always hated the Russian girl, and they had a list of reasons why, ending with a particular TV station. "Hey, bitch," I greet her, pulling Taya's attention away from the classmate she'd been talking to.

With a hearty chuckle, she pulls me into a hug. "Haven't seen you in a couple days, Vana. Where have you been?"

"Busy with school." I wish I had some fanciful tale to weave. At least that I'd had a hot date more recently than a year ago. But I was never one to embellish. "Waiting for Papa to pick me up. You're more than welcome to join us."

She snickers. "Yes, I'm sure they would love that."

"Oh, come on. They haven't been nearly as bad about you since we split up."

"Your mother told me to get in line if I wanted any bread."

I do my best not to laugh. Really, I do. Perhaps I'm too used to my mother's sense of humor, or maybe it really was a good joke. "It wasn't even good bread."

"No. No it wasn't." She rolls her eyes, slinging her backpack from her shoulder and gesturing toward a bench. There's light foot traffic around campus and a few people smoking in a gazebo, so there's not much to observe from our new seat. A squirrel scurries over to investigate a piece of an apple on the ground, looks at us, and runs away.

I sigh, slumping and stretching my legs out. "Do you have much homework?"

She rolls her eyes. "Same as ever. Are you trying to avoid something?"

I shrug.

"Today's the day, isn't it? Your weird superstitious thing."

I nod.

"That why you're seeing your parents?"

"What? No." I stare at her. "I see them every Wednesday."

Her hand darts up to brush an errant strand of dark brown hair from her eyes. "I forgot about that."

"Have you heard from yours recently?"

Taya shakes her head, studying the bit of apple. "Not in a few weeks. Time difference and all that."

"Of course."

She shrugs. "I met a new girl."

Righting myself, I gape at her. It's not that I'm jealous—at least any more than a nostalgic twinge—I've never seen her show any interest in anyone else. "Congrats," I offer nonchalantly.

"Don't worry. It's no one you know."

"Why would I worry about that?"

"I thought you wouldn't want me stealing your meager options. I know how long it can take you to work up the nerve to make a move on a girl. Wouldn't want to interrupt that process."

"It was a week!"

"A week of me practically throwing myself at you."

"Still only a week. And I didn't even see you for half of it."

"I'm pretty sure we saw each other every day that week. Class hadn't started yet."

"Well…" Damn, she's right. "You could've asked me."

"I did. You misunderstood."

I grumble. "Clearly, your accent was too thick."

With a snort, she spits back, "I'm sure that's all it was."

"Wasn't sure if you were asking me for some vodka or a date."

"I don't think any accent would do that."

"It was the first Russian stereotype I could think of."

She leans in, and her hand settles on my shoulder as she meets my eyes, a deadly serious expression on her face. "You need to ask your mother for help making better Russian jokes."

To avoid acknowledging her, I take out my flip phone. A text from my father says that he's on his way, and the clock reads 5:05. So I can't yet make my escape. "Well, you'll have to introduce me to your new girl." At least it moves the topic safely away from my own terrible dating skills.

"If things get serious, I'm sure I'll have to introduce you eventually." Her broad grin belies her nonchalance. She really does like this girl. Despite the twinge of jealousy—though I'm not sure if it's of her or the mysterious woman—I really am happy for her.

"What's her name?"

"Stephanie."

"Wow, she's not even Slavic."

"You'll live."

"I don't know if that's true."

Taya sighs. "That's how you know you're Russian. All those depressed remarks. If you had a bit more vodka, you'd sound exactly like any of our poets."

If there's one thing that my parents taught me... "Call me Russian again, and I'll show you what I learned in that kickboxing class last year."

"Saturday?"

"For meeting the Canadian girl or for our fight?"

"Both, probably."

I wish I had to check my schedule. "Yeah, I'm free." My phone buzzes with a new text. *I'm here.* He's early. "And with that, I'd best be off."

"Give your parents a proper red hello from their old nemesis."

"Sure, I'll tell them you called them comrades."

"That should work."

I give her a quick peck on the cheek, scoop my bag off the ground, and run a couple blocks toward my dorm.

Chapter Two

Roze

A lonesome baby cries in the woods. It calls to me. Our other duties have begun to fall by the wayside as society has moved on, but children will always grow lost. And we'll always be there.

This one was lost through no fault of its mother's. She desires not gold nor power, only her child returned. I know this as surely as I know my woods.

I arrive on my own, swept along by its need for protection. I travel without my mother today. I have for many years now. It's a strange change, though I've had time to grow accustomed to it, but as a child, I always expected to arrive as one of three. Remaining a trio is not unheard of, I've even done so, but it's not so common as I'd once thought.

The pitiful thing wails as I approach. "Don't fear, child. I'm here. All will be all right." I scoop him into my arms, brushing a finger along the apple-round cheek. "I could just eat you up."

He squeaks and babbles back at me, drooling on my hand.

"Your mother will be along soon. She's worried sick about you." And looking for him. She's near, stepping into my woods. In a moment, I'll have to return him.

Despite what the mothers always fear—what I know people say—I've never felt the slightest urge to steal one of the children in my care. We don't replace them with brooms or whatever that story claimed. That was all paranoid women trying to look a gift horse in the mouth. Humans who would stop at nothing to distrust us.

Children are our calling. We know their futures, care for the lost, and save those from parents who care not for them.

Her foot falls in my woods, and I feel it. I knew the mother wouldn't be long. The baby babbles over my shoulder as I weave between the trees, knowing every twist and turn of the path to reach her.

There she is. A slight thing, with dark hair and a feeble body. I'm surprised she was able to give birth. "Paulinus," she calls, holding a light as her gaze rakes over my woods.

"I have him." My voice is soft and cool; there's no reason to alarm her. Her intentions are pure. The little child—Paulinus—crawled off while she smoked meat. Its scent wafts over. Meat, hardly my preference. I hope she doesn't expect me to take some in thanks.

She turns, her light shining right in my eye. Squinting, I see her jaw drop as she stammers something unintelligible.

"Your child is fine." I hold him out and receive an annoyed gurgle for my trouble.

The woman stares at the baby. "It's…but you're…" Fortunately, she thinks enough to shine the light somewhere other than my face, illuminating the dirt and rocks at our feet.

I nod.

Her foot digs into the ground. She'll twist her ankle if she tries to run. I can see it, hear the snap, feel the pain.

"Lift your foot up, there's a root right there. You'll trip."

In her confusion, she does trip but catches herself. There's no snap. "But…why would you—"

"I'm merely here to return your child."

"How do I know it's my child?" She looks like she wants to scream it but is simply too scared. Normally, my visage is more comforting than that of my sisters. I glance down and see my hands and feet are still those of humans. It's only the tales that frighten her. "You're a laume. I know what you do."

I lean forward, extending the child and risking my balance should she attempt to attack me. Others have before. But it's a sign of trust, and I hope she'll see it as that rather than as an opening. "Please. You know your boy. This is your Paulinus."

Darting forward, she snatches the infant from my hands before retreating again, her eyes wide as she stares at me.

Gold appears in my hand, sifting through my fingers, falling to my feet, embedding itself in the dirt. There's powder, bars, coins, jewelry, it's all the same to us. "You're a sick and overworked mother, raising the child on your own. Take this, and may it ease your burdens."

She continues to stare, no words leaving her mouth.

"You have nothing to fear from me. You are a good mother who simply needs a helping hand. You didn't seek in greed or wile. Take the gold. It is a gift, and you owe me nothing in return. Simply care for your child as he deserves."

Her gaze falls to the cooing baby before darting back to me, scared and expecting me to lunge. What stories has she heard? The changeling rumor I understand, but is she scared that I'll pinch and tweak her to death? "Thank you," she stammers.

"You owe me no thanks." The last of the gold falls at her feet, and I walk away, letting my woods take me in. The child will grow to be a politician; a scandal will nearly unseat him, but he'll devote himself anew and turn Klaipeda into the most prosperous town it's been since Germans first took an interest in it. While I have somewhere I must be.

CHAPTER THREE

DOVANA

The garage door closes, leaving us in an overly packed two-car garage with barely enough room for the single car. "I can smell your mother's cooking already," my father says.

It isn't true. The kitchen is halfway across the house, with a good three walls in the way, and the car doors are still closed. Despite this, I'm almost hungry enough to agree. I should've had more than that bagel this morning.

He opens the door to the house, letting me in first, and now I really can smell it. The scents of spiced meat, frying oil, and crisping potatoes perfume the air. My favorite. "You didn't tell me we were having potato pancakes."

"He wanted to save it as a surprise," my mother calls from the other room. "I trust it's a pleasant one."

"It is!"

My little brother's footsteps sound down the hall toward the bedrooms. "Oh, you're here." Matis stares at me, bright blue eyes shining up from messy blond hair.

"Is that how we say hello now?" Papa asks.

"Hi, Vana," he mutters, heading toward the kitchen.

I muss his hair as I follow. "Nice to see you too, Matis," The brat.

"There's some gira in the fridge," Mama says.

My ears perk up. She hasn't made my favorite drink in years. Am I in trouble? Am I being rewarded? It's the middle of the semester, so grades couldn't have been sent out...what happened? "With strawberries?" I ask.

"Make sure before you pour it. There's one with raisins in it too."

Blegh. Raisins. I tentatively sniff one of the sealed carafes on the top shelf, as the opening is too small to tell what's floating in it, and I am not willing to risk exposure to the foul food. Mostly, it smells like beer but breadier. There's the faintest hint of strawberry, however, so I take a risk and pour it in a large glass.

"Want any?" I ask no one in particular.

"Yeah," Matis calls from his seat at the table.

"Then at least set the table, and I'll pour you one."

Grumbling, he pulls himself back to his feet and to the cupboards.

Oil bubbles as another pancake splashes into the pan. "How many are you going to want?" my mother asks.

Ten. "Like, three."

She studies the nearly empty bowl of mashed potatoes. "There should be just enough for you to have four."

Score. "Thanks, Mama." I set the drinks on the table before thinking better of it and heading back to get the gross kind for my parents. I know raisins barely affect the flavor, but I don't know how they can stomach it. It's like having dead bugs in your drink. Though any time I have voiced that concern, she says that they called that an extra treat when she was a kid.

My brother finishes setting the table and sits across from me while my father sits to my right, sipping idly at his drink. "You need any help, honey?"

"No, we're all done." She sets a plate piled high with potato pancakes and a heaping helping of cabbage at the center of the table and sits across from my papa. "Dig in, everyone. Good potato."

Matis snickers. He loves how much he has corrupted our perfectly innocent language. Just because he had to learn English first and couldn't manage to pronounce it on his first try, now we always have to say it. I glare at him as menacingly as I can manage while I fork my dinner onto my plate. They're as crisp and perfect as ever, the golden skin like a mouthwatering french fry, barely containing the pork and onion mixture. Before anyone can say anything more, I help myself. Maybe I'm simply starving, but I swear she's never made them better. I wish I really could have ten.

"How was school?" Mama asks, spreading butter on hers.

"It was fine," Matis and I both reply.

I gesture for him to go first so I can focus on my food and maybe even snatch up an extra pancake. "The teacher started reading a new book—it's really good—something about a milk carton, and we had to start doing math where the answer doesn't go at the end after the equal mark. It's really weird."

"You're doing algebra?" our father asks.

He shrugs.

"How're you picking it up?"

He shrugs again. "It's all right. Just weird."

"What about you, Dovana?" Mama asks.

"We went over de Beauvoir's ideas of female empowerment and discussed the reading from a chapter of *The Second Sex*. And in my morning class, I got to learn about how everything is fire. Which I'm sure made cooking the food a lot easier."

"What?"

"It's part of what led up to the idea of the four elements," I explain, wiping food from my lips with a cloth napkin. "One of the early ideas was that there was only fire. It was basically a metaphor for change." I'd actually really enjoyed the lesson, but it's quickly dawning on me that I should not be a teacher. I have no idea how to convey it in such a way that it will make sense to anyone who doesn't already love the ideas of Greek philosophy. They had about the same reaction when I tried explaining the allegory of the cave.

"Well, I'm glad you're enjoying it," Papa says.

"It's really interesting."

"Have you thought any more about what you're going to do with your degree?" My mother sounds worried. It's not like I need to worry about the money. Not that she has ever been able to relax enough to really enjoy that.

I chew on my lip, the last pancake on my plate looking slightly less appetizing. Not a lot less, I'm still gonna eat it, but a little. "I'm still not sure."

"What do philosophers do these days?" my father asks.

"Bitch about things and teach?"

"Dovana!" my mother snaps.

My cheeks burn. Right, no cursing in front of the baby.

"It's not like I don't know what 'bitch' means," he says.

Her eyes burn into me. I'm not the one who taught him. I only taught him to curse in Lithuanian. "It's these Canadian public schools," I say. "You know how they are. They ruined me after my proper upbringing, and now they're doing the same to this poor boy. Oh, if only something could be done."

"Dovana," she repeats.

I offer back a smile.

She rolls her eyes. "Eat your food."

"And don't think this worked as a trick to avoid the question either," my father says.

Damn, that would've been brilliant. I wish I'd thought of it. "I talked to my guidance counselor about job prospects." I hadn't wanted to tell them about it since I hadn't really liked any of the ideas, but if it'll get them to let me eat in peace, then anything is worth it. I swear, it's not like I ask them about their prospects. And I'm the one who paid for everything in the first place. Well, Roze is. But she gave the money to me. I think.

"And what did he say?" Mama asks.

"She. Really, Mama, I can't believe you. Just because you're a housewife doesn't mean—"

"Dovana."

I swallow, going pale. She hates being called that. She had started as a physics instructor at what ended up being my college when Matis was born. When he was three, she decided to focus on raising him...and me, I suppose, as I was a moody teenager at the time and had to be plenty of work myself. She doesn't take kindly to being attacked for that choice.

"Sorry. She said that a philosophy degree is really useful to prepare for a lot of other jobs—including a bunch of white-collar stuff, which mostly sounded awful—but also higher education. Since grad school is mostly about doing even more reading than I am right now, being used to interpreting big unwieldy texts is a rather marketable skill. I could go and be a doctor, a psychologist, a vet, a lawyer, maybe a pharmacist. All that stuff." I'm not sure what sounds most appealing from those. Honestly, I'd want to be a tattoo artist if I wasn't horrible at art and if besmirching my perfect skin wouldn't send my mother to the ICU.

"Really?" Papa asks. "That's wonderful. I'd assumed it was going to be a dead-end, useless degree."

I scoff. "Gee, thanks."

"I didn't mean—"

"He says it a lot," Matis cuts in. "He's worried you're, what was it, dooming your projects?"

"Prospects," he grumbles.

I gape at him. "You said that? Why? What?" I grind my teeth, stabbing my fork into the remaining half a pancake and stuffing the entire thing in my mouth. "I'm going to figure everything out. You don't need to worry. I'll have enough money either way."

"You can't rely on a fairy to give you everything," my mother insists, her voice remaining calm despite her obvious agitation. She's said it so many times but rarely in an actual argument.

"You're in trouble," Matis talk-sings.

I stick my tongue out at him before turning back to my mother. "I've been smart with my money. I still have enough to live on after college even if she never gives me any more gold."

"And what if it all disappears?"

"Mama, you know she's not like that. Hell, they're not like that. We're not Irish. They're not tricksters. I can take care of myself, and if, big if, for some reason, that did happen, then I'd find a job or get student loans. It'd be okay."

She sighs but nods.

"Speaking of, since you're already being so nice to Roze, do you have any rye bread?"

She shakes her head. "You're drinking it."

Damn. I drain the rest of my gira. I might as well have more of it if that was all our rye. "Well, it won't be authentic kepta duona then, but how about honey wheat? Last year, I left her that and some milk, and the letter treated it as the most amazing thing she'd ever eaten."

"We could go to the store and get some," Papa said. "The one right around the corner is still open."

She waves him off. "That shouldn't be necessary. It's a little stale, but it should be perfect for frying." Her chair squeaks on the tiles as she slides back and ambles to the kitchen, opening the little shelf high above the oven and pulling out a wrapped artisanal loaf. "I was going to make some pudding with it, but I can buy some more." She gives it a once-over, checking for mold before setting it before me on the table. "Need anything else? Do you even have milk in your fridge?"

I want to snap at her, but I have to admit, "I don't, could you put some in a thermos?"

"Of course. Just remind me before you go. Or you could bring over some gira with it. I'm sure she wouldn't mind the raisin kind," she adds, grabbing the pitcher from the fridge and refilling my empty glass.

"That's perfect. Thank you. Yes, I'll set some out for her."

"Happy to help." She smirks.

"I want to see a fairy," Matis mutters.

"Don't call her that," Papa says, nudging him under the table.

"She said it first!"

"And I shouldn't have."

He crosses his arms.

"You gonna eat that?" I ask, gesturing at his plate and its remaining pancake.

"Yes!"

"Just asking." I smile as innocently as I can manage.

He rolls his eyes and proceeds to eat the entire thing, staring right at me.

We all keep at it for a bit, talking, more relaxed now that they don't think I'm throwing my life away, and enjoying our food. My mother even stuffs some of those little mushroom cookies I love in my bag. Thankfully, they're not made with real mushrooms, simply shaped like it. I probably love them because they remind me of her. And because they're delicious.

❖

I lean back in my bed, sipping at a thermos of decidedly not-raisined gira. Caroline munches on one of my cookies in her own bed. "Did you have fun?"

I nod, lacing my fingers behind my head. I'll fry the bread up when she's going to bed. That way, she won't notice me setting it out. I'm not making that mistake again. "It's always nice seeing them. And having my mama's cooking. Like, oh my God, that potato pancake was to die for."

"What's a potato pancake?"

I stare at her, my jaw practically hitting the floor. "You've never had a potato pancake?"

She shakes her head.

"Well, I'm just going to have to fix that." I grin. "I'll see about getting my mother's recipe."

"No offense, Vana, but I've had your cooking before."

"Offense taken, and this will be better. I hadn't made grilled cheese before."

"Have you made potato pancakes before?"

"Well, no."

She chuckles. "And is it going to involve frying and setting our kitchen on fire?"

"I didn't set it on fire."

"There was a fire on the stove."

"That's where fire is supposed to go."

"Not in the center of it."

I stare at the wall. Now would probably be a terrible time to bring up that I'm about to fry. "Well, I'll practice first."

"Not here."

"It's my apartment too."

"Fine, but if we have to call the fire department, you owe me twenty bucks."

"Then I'm just not going to call the fire department."

She lets out a low groan, holding her head. "That is not inspiring confidence, Vana."

"It'll be fine. I cooked with Mama a month ago and didn't even burn the food. I can manage."

With another exasperated sigh, she pulls herself to her feet, shaking her head. "Well, I'm going to go get ready for bed. You going to sleep?"

Maybe I can cook while she's in the bath. Then she might not even notice. "Not for a little while."

"Wanna watch our show when I'm done? I'd be up for an episode before bed."

I smile up at her. "Sure, that sounds great."

As soon as she closes the door behind her, I leap up and get to work, setting sunflower oil in a frying pan over a hot burner and slicing up the honey wheat loaf into little fingers. By the time I hear her turn off the water and settle into the tub, I'm already rubbing cloves of garlic over the bread. My mama always makes a cheese sauce for it, but I didn't think to buy mayonnaise, so she's gonna have to deal with only having garlic and salt. I take a bite to see how bad her sacrifice will be. Wow, I actually managed to cook something good. Roze will absolutely love them. It's just nice being able to actually do something for her. Even if I can't see her.

I eat three of the little sticks before I catch myself. This isn't for me. Wrapping it in a napkin, I open the window, and along with the thermos of gira, a pen, and a letter I wrote while I meant to do homework, I set it on the window sill. There's barely enough room, but it all stays in place, and I manage to close the window and settle in to actually do my homework until Caroline finishes her bath.

Chapter Four

Roze

Something smells amazing. It calls to me.

Every year. She keeps doing this. I wish I could find it in me to tell her to stop, but I'm not sure I'd be able to take it. I'd lose my mind if I stopped hearing from her. It'd break my heart.

Especially with how this one smells. It's like the honey loaf from before—which everyone should give to all fair folk all the time—but with a few other scents mixed in. Mostly oil and garlic.

The park a few blocks away hardly counts as woods anymore, let alone the forest I'd prefer, but it's enough that I can step out of it. Seeing the city never grows any more normal. These towers of stone, steel, and glass are unlike anything in my world. I can't imagine how the humans manage.

Narrowly avoiding a speeding metal—what're they called? Death machine will have to do, as I can't recall. I cross the kilometer or so to her.

The offering is set a good distance up, but that means little to me. I wasn't lucky as to be born with wings, but I can climb as well as anyone else who's spent their entire life surrounded by trees.

They smell even more amazing up close. She made this for me. I take a seat on the sill, ready to have a look at her offering, when I hear noises inside.

She's still awake. Normally, she doesn't set my offering out until she goes to bed. Heedless of the risk of falling, I lean over, doing my best to peer in. There are blinds obstructing the view, but I can see lights and her talking to another woman. The future slams into me as sudden and frightening as Dovana's always is. I falter, teetering on the edge, but I manage to keep my balance.

How is it that after all these years, it's still unchanged? I've done everything. By the rainbow, there has to be a better way.

Sulkily, I sip the drink she left out. It tastes like bread. I love bread.

I drain half of it before setting it beside me and picking up her letter. She's left me one each year since we were children. It's the only way I can really say that we're friends. I wish I could spend time with her, have gotten to know her like I'd have liked—as scary as humans are, she never seemed it—and maybe then, I'd have her to count on.

I chew on the crisp honey-garlic bread, which, wow, oh my God, everyone should make some and leave it on their window for me. I open the letter one-handed and start reading.

Dear Roze,

Happy Anniversary. It's been fifteen years now. You're my oldest friend, now that I think about it. I said that to Mama earlier, and I realized it's true. The only other people I knew back in Lithuania disappeared from my life years ago.

I hope you like the food. I used honey wheat. I know how much you loved it last time.

I've had an exhausting year. I don't think I've done anything but read. Taking four higher level philosophy classes was probably a bad idea. But I'm really loving them. Thank you for talking me into taking it as my major. My guidance counselor told me a bunch of stuff that I can do with it, and I think I've mostly convinced my parents that it's not career suicide.

How about you? Has your mother finally come around to letting you go work on your own? Did you ever figure out what was up with those ziburinis *encroaching on your forest? Personally, I'd love* to see some glowing skeletons, but I'm sure they're way scarier in person. I hope you managed to work things out with them. Or kicked their asses if you had to. Wow, I'm just realizing how insensitive this could sound if something happened with them. I'm tempted to just delete this part, but I really want to know what happened, and if I can't stick my foot in my mouth talking to my oldest friend, then who can I do so with? (Sorry, I couldn't resist.)

Oh, right! I'd told you about Taya, right? I think you managed to miss our entire relationship, but she and I started becoming friends again around my last letter, so I'm not sure if I mentioned any of that. It had really seemed like she was going to be gone from my life for good a couple years ago, and now I talk to her almost every day. It's weird. How about you? Have you finally met someone? Maybe you ended up with a ziburini, and I'm extra insensitive. Please say you're not dating a skeleton. Can they even have sex? How would they do it? If you are, I want details!

I sigh, leaning back against the wall. I wish I could be with someone. Not that a ziburini would be my first choice.

She goes on about her classes for a little while, recommends some book by some philosopher. I enjoy the occasional human book, and I suppose I can give this one a shot. Her last recommendation was surprisingly mesmerizing.

After her rambling, she signs it by calling herself my oldest friend and adds a quick p.s. to let her know if I like the gira even with raisins.

I do, so I'll make sure to include it in my response.

I angle myself so that I can write on the wall and pull out the letter I wrote on a thin-woven linen parchment. I try to always add a response on top of my main letter.

I write,

The bread was absolutely amazing, as was the gira. If you include it next time, I'll be eternally grateful.

I'm happy to hear that you and Taya are better friends, though you actually had mentioned that you were talking again last time.

Sorry that your studies have been so intense, but I'm glad to hear that you seem to be doing well. I have not met anyone, the ziburinis have kept to themselves and have been displaced by a logging company. No, I don't think they can have sex, but I've never particularly wanted to attempt to find out.

The light goes out inside, and the sound dies away. I guess she's finally going to sleep.

Sweet dreams, Vana.
Friends forever,
Roze

I slip the letter under the window, just enough for it to stay in place. Then I finish my food and climb back down. I didn't want to risk waking her when I left, and figured it was safer this way. I wish I could actually talk to her.

As I step onto the ground—if you can even call it that—I shake my head. I know why I can't. I can't let the future happen.

I leave her to her dreams and philosophy and head to the nearest book store. They'll never miss a single copy.

Chapter Five

Dovana

Her. God. Damn. Alarm.

She's already snoozed it once. I swear, one of these days, I'm going to turn her alarm off when she sleeps. I'm not sure it'd actually teach her a lesson, but at least I'd get a full night's sleep for the first weeknight in months.

But I have a reason to be up this time. As soon as she heads to the bathroom, I open the window, grabbing the letter before it slips down.

Coins start spilling onto my sheets and don't stop. More than could possibly have fit in the pages. As the bathroom door opens, I toss the sheets over the pile, hoping that the strange lump in the bed isn't too noticeable, and do my best to sit comfortably on the pile of gold.

"Oh, you're awake." She stares, her hand on her hip, having already put on jeans, a T-shirt, and a bit of lipstick.

I nod. "You woke me up."

"Sorry."

I've told her so many times. "Would you please just not snooze your alarm? I can go back to sleep way more easily if you only use it the one time."

She throws her hands up. "I can't wake up the first time. We've been over this. I don't know what you want from me."

She really isn't that bad of a roommate. This early class of hers is killing me. "Please at least try." I shift, the coins jingle, so I try yawning, hoping that will somehow make enough noise to cover it. If I wore a necklace, then the sound could be justified. "I would appreciate it."

Crossing her arms, she stares at her bed and gives a noncommittal shrug.

I wish I could talk to her about things, but I can't take that risk again. I'm not letting her think I'm crazy, and I'm doubly not letting her try to exploit Roze for gold. Though, granted, that would just get her baby killed. Though she doesn't have a baby, so I'm not actually sure what would happen. Why are westerners always so bad at understanding this sort of stuff anyway? Don't they have that Shakespeare quote about heaven and earth to rely on? I still have way too much of Hamlet memorized from my class last semester. Oh well, it's clearly not worth it. Not like Russians are much better. Why did we ever move?

Caroline heads to the door and opens it, turning around at the last moment with the most awkward little grin on her face. "Your classes end at four, right?"

"Yes, though I have one that ends at two, so I usually grab a bite before my three o'clock one. Why?"

Her fingers tap out a quick beat on the wooden door. "Could you maybe not come back until five?"

I stare at her. "I live here too."

"*Please.*"

I groan. I'm about ready to agree to get her out so I can hide my gold, but it's the principle of the thing. "Why?"

Another rhythm, faster this time, with her smile growing all the more nervous and forced. Her hand darts to her hair, tucking a strand behind her ear. "I have this guy coming over," she says in a monotone, as if it doesn't mean anything.

"Uh-huh."

"And I mean, you can of course have a girl over whenever. I'd make sure you had alone time. And he doesn't live on campus, so this is when he's free. And I kind of like him, and he's really hot. Seriously, you should see his abs."

I shrug.

"Please."

"Please look at his abs?"

She rolls her eyes.

"Will you stop snoozing your alarm?"

She groans. "You're mean."

"Well, maybe I'll just have to head here for lunch after class."

"Fine. I'll stop snoozing it. At least, I'll try harder. But stay out of here until at least six then."

"You said five."

Her eyes narrow. "Vana!"

"Yes, yes." I chuckle. "Fine. I'll be back around six. Want me to grab dinner?"

She blinks. It's still early, and planning out dinner seems impossibly far away. "Pizza? I'll pay you back."

"Sure, I'll see what slices they have. I know what you like."

"Yeah, because I eat there like twice a week." She sighs and checks her watch. "Well, I need to get going. Thanks for making me late." A far more playful glare flashes on her face. "See you tonight. Love you."

"You too. See you then."

The second the door locks behind her, I pull back the sheet. The coins have at least stopped appearing, so I should hopefully be able to finally read my letter. I stuff everything in the safe I keep in the bottom drawer of my desk—I can't exactly deposit my magic fairy money in a bank—lock it, and take a seat at my computer, the letter clutched in my hand.

I really want to go back to sleep, but I'm thoroughly awake at this point.

My Dearest Dovana Gudaite. How does she still write like that? This isn't the 1800s.

It finally happened. It's only been a few days since I last saw you, so it will hardly be fresh by the time you read it, but Mother actually let me work on my own. There was a lost child—reminded me of a certain someone who shall remain nameless—and I had to help her find her parents. They were out hiking in these woods in Russia. Now, I know how you feel about Russians, but the poor dear was about to freeze to death when I found her. I had to carry her several kilometers up a steep slope before I finally located them. They were so relieved to see her and didn't seem at all bothered by my presence. Maybe laume stories have finally spread farther than the Baltic Sea. They thanked me profusely, gave me some of their snacks, and warmed the poor dear up by the fire.

Until now, I never knew how much I actually love the work we do. Sure, I've saved plenty of people and made interesting friends before, but that was all in my mother's shadow. I didn't hate it, but it was simply a thing that I did because of who and what I was. Other laume have taken other specialties. They don't all call the forests home. Some have even taken bathhouses and started more than a few scandalous myths. I could have easily decided to pursue something different if I'd wanted to. I'm not sure the thought ever entirely crossed my head, but now that I'm finally doing this for myself, I know that it never will.

I'll still sew and tend as needed, but saving the lost children, it's the greatest calling one can have.

Squeezed in next to it, she added, *Your education is of course still wonderful too.*

Since then, I've had far more to do. The other duties still take up some of my time, but I've had so much to do in just my true pursuit. I hope that you're able to find something that means as much to you. If you end up really enjoying those psychology classes, then you could help people too. That would be wonderful.

I forgot that I was considering a psych major last year. Maybe if that high-pitched creep hadn't been my first instructor, I'd have been more interested in keeping with it. Now I feel kind of bad. Will any of my career prospects be that meaningful?

I don't mean to brag, but I've had so many people desperate to thank me after I saved their family. It's not why I do it, but it never seemed to happen to my mother. I'm not sure if she avoided it or what. Maybe I'm doing something wrong. I was invited for dinner the other day in thanks for bringing a child home. People lose their children so often! The food was great, though it wasn't as good as that honey bread you brought me last year. If you don't leave that out this time, please do so next year again. Please.

I can't help but roll my eyes. God, she loves honey wheat so much. I'm glad I decided to fry it for her. I wonder if she preferred that or if I should take the lazy option and give her a store-bought loaf next time, like I have before.

She goes on for a while, detailing all of the various rescues she's been involved in. I'm a little surprised to find that my cheeks hurt from how broadly I've been smiling. She sounds so happy. I'm not sure I've ever heard her anywhere near this excited. I wonder if anything will ever make me feel quite that way.

I glance at the time on my laptop to find that I really need to start getting ready for school. She wrote nearly an entire novel. I can take the letter with me and read more later. I have a whole year to reply, after all.

I take a quick shower, throw on jeans and a T-shirt—and underwear, but that's not as visible—grab my bags, and dash across the campus. There's still enough time, but it's on the other side of campus, and I'd rather not take the risk.

The professor doesn't show up until five minutes after class is supposed to start. It's not uncommon, but it's annoying. We have a lot of material to cover, and I'd much rather have him go over everything and maybe even have time to review. There's a test next week, and I want to be ready.

He's nearly the Platonic form of a college professor, straight down to the tweed jacket, and when class finally starts, he gesticulates wildly at his PowerPoint with a laser pointer, sending it all over the screen as he talks. Most of this is going back over stuff I already knew—ancient philosophy has a lot of the same thinkers as introductory philosophy—but it all feels much more overwhelming now. At least it gives me an excuse to use terms like Platonic forms. That's always fun.

As he begins discussing Diogenes, my mind starts to wander. Appropriate when covering a homeless man.

Something about the letter just keeps clinging to me. I hadn't even thought of it at the time, but there was something wrong. And it wasn't its ungodly length. I'm used to that by now between her and my classes. It was something more.

"Behold a man," the professor shouts, telling one of the most overused philosophy jokes and one that he told when we first went over Diogenes. Maybe he's trying to get people to pay attention. Right, I should do that. I turn my gaze back to him, typing out a quick note from the slide.

She visited them for tea.

Not only the kid she rescued but her whole family. She talked to them, ate with them.

Why didn't she do that for us?

As soon as she saw my parents, she disappeared and never showed up again, save for her letters. I'd assumed that was just how laumes were. They showed up for the job, and then they left. It was always how her mother sounded in her letters, so it made sense. Why would they even want to associate with humans? I had kind of assumed I was special.

Does she write letters to everyone? As long as mine are, that doesn't seem likely. She wouldn't have enough time in the day. But why does she refuse to see me? She's my friend, and I'd love to be able to see her more often. I spend all year looking forward to these letters.

How can she visit other people?

"Yes, that's generally agreed to be one of the dialogues that was exclusively Plato, rather than actually being based on Socrates's ideas. There's a good bit of confusion on the subject, but it's one of the later ones, so we're mostly certain of this. Thank you for that point. It doesn't get brought up nearly enough."

Wait, we moved on already? How long have I been spacing out? Damn it, I have to be ready for this test. This is one of the hardest classes I have, and I still don't know why. I'm not messing up this test. I only got a B last time. Come on, Dovana, focus. You have a whole year to worry about Roze.

But why does it have to be a year?

It's only been every year because I've always done it to honor the anniversary. I guess I was a really sentimental kid.

She visits other people without any special occasion. I know I am jealous, but I'm more confused. Why would she not visit me? Should I try inviting her for tea or dinner? She didn't stick around long enough last time, but I could include it in the next letter. It would mean having to wait a whole year for my answer.

"…Aristotle's school."

I've missed almost the entire review. I shake my head, tapping a few keys on my keyboard. I only have three lines of notes. If I didn't know any better, I'd think she was trying to make me fail.

He covers the last of the review. My mind almost manages to stay with it, and I jot down a little more, but I'll have to go online and look at his slides or ask a classmate what I missed. I never do this. I'm a good student. I pride myself on it. I never let my life interfere. I can't believe I did this.

The class lets out, and I sulk out to the hall, disappointed in myself as can be. I have a long break, so I can grab some food, go over the slideshow, and still have time to get a bit farther in the letter before my next class. I just need to focus.

Chapter Six

Roze

The grass is cool beneath me, and the clouds drift idly overhead through slits in the foliage. No child calls out for me. I have a moment to rest and think.

A copy of *Edifying Discourses in Diverse Spirit* sits on my lap. It's not the one that she recommended I read, but Dovana had mentioned a few times how much she was enjoying the workings of Soren Kierkegaard's mind. What better way into hers than through his?

If I could only manage to find my way through it.

I should've grabbed a copy in Lithuanian.

English is my fourth language, and while I had thought myself prolific in it, this text is making me increasingly question that conviction. I think I've gone over this paragraph three times already, and I find myself no closer to understanding what it's trying to impart to me. I'm only on the second page.

A particular word jumps out at me. That may be because it appears three times in a single sentence, and the sentence includes other words also referring to it, but I don't feel as if that's the only reason it's on my mind. The future. Perhaps this is why she enjoys him so; he's able to conjure up exactly what she's thinking. If that is what he's saying. I'm not quite certain. Why did I think an English philosophy book was a good idea?

If only I could grab hold of the future's manifold varieties, as I'm reasonably certain this book says one can. If only the future even had manifold varieties. I've tried everything I can think of. It has been fifteen years. How has her fate not once faltered? I've changed fates like few others before me.

Nothing big, of course. I'm not foolish as to ignore the ripples that could cause. But I've prevented deaths, avoided accidents and injuries. I even once stopped a couple from breaking up by pointing out how each had misheard the other. I hadn't happened upon them by chance. They were fighting because their child was lost. It's my main way of meeting people.

So what is it about this girl? She doesn't have any great destiny. She isn't some queen or prophet. She's just a girl. Why is her fate so intractable?

I try to force myself on to the second sentence, hoping that it'll clarify the prior and the quagmire I find myself in. Not that I've ever escaped it.

"Even if it does not deserve the name of love, it still ought not be dismissed as thoughtlessness." I just got called out by a dead man. Wow.

Maybe that's not calling out my actions so much as condoning them? I have to translate it all in my head as I think, and it grows increasingly complex. I don't love her, at least not as more than a friend, no matter what her future may suggest, but I've always feared that she may see my protecting her as mere thoughtlessness. But am I now only using the words of someone she idolizes as an excuse for hiding the truth from her? Am I really even protecting her or simply myself? I wonder what good old Soren would have to say on this matter.

The book finally starts to make a semblance of sense as I bury myself in it, taking the better part of an hour to read the first chapter, going over and over each line, making sure that I've wrung them for every last drop of meaning. Is this why she enjoys her new pursuit? Perhaps I could learn to find it fulfilling as well. Maybe it will even give me something to talk about with her in my next letter. Assuming she keeps the major this time.

Chuckling at my own joke, I stare at the forest around me and find that I'm no longer alone. "Mother, you're here."

Her cloven hooves produce only a dull thud as she strides across the grass, her serene face smiling. "You wanted to see me, did you not?"

I nod. It has been weighing on me, and if anyone would know, then it would have to be her. And it's always nice to see her.

"Was anything the matter? Or could you simply not wait until supper tomorrow?"

With a heavy sigh, I stuff the book into the bag that holds its sibling. "I just wanted to talk to you. It wasn't anything urgent."

Sitting on her haunches before me, she gives me that knowing look, the one that says there's more than I'm saying. I'm sure most mothers have one. "That hardly sounds true, my dear flower. What's on your mind?"

I interlace my fingers behind my head, leaning back against a tree as I study her. I've kept this a secret for fifteen long years, should I...*no, don't be ridiculous*. If I told her, it would be as bad as letting it happen. "It's about our seer powers, Mother."

"This again?" She props herself up on one forearm, peering into my eyes. I do my best to look relaxed and unbothered. "I know you have a certain gift for it, but I've never understood why you obsess on it so."

Maybe I should try to make like a philosopher. If I treat it as a thought experiment, then perhaps the truth will seem less obvious. "What is it that determines what we can change? I've never been clear on it. I've seen futures and had no trouble altering them, but then other times, it seems that they're simply meant to be. Is there some guiding force that I'm missing, and if so, why does it work on others?" That doesn't sound theoretical enough. "Does it have something to do with their beliefs, perhaps? I've simply always been so curious." Better.

Rather than looking as if I've asked an interesting theoretical quandary, she appears concerned. "This seems to always be on your mind. Is there something in particular you're trying to change?"

I do my best to wave off her fears. "Of course not. I've just always wondered. Like, I saved a woman from breaking her leg when she saw me the other day, and it wasn't as if the future changed back to her injuring herself another way, but other times, I've seen people who were destined to fall in love, and it seemed that no matter how things around them changed, they were still meant to be. Are there different kinds of destiny?"

"Why would you try to prevent people from falling in love?"

Maybe that wasn't the best example. "Not me, just in general."

She cocks her head. "Love is very complicated. It's not as simple as cause and effect. You can change a minor thing and expect to prevent injury or even illness, but that doesn't mean that two people won't fall in love. If they're meant to be, they're simply meant to be. Or if there isn't any higher cause, then two people who have great chemistry one day will still have it the next day. Now, are you—"

"What about life or death?" I don't want to talk about love. I know exactly what I can expect there. I'll find another fair one I can breed with and continue our race. There's nothing to discuss. It doesn't matter what I want. It doesn't matter how unsure I am of what I want. I have a duty to my people, and I will fulfill that.

"That can be as simple as an injury. Or as complex as anything else. Could you tell me what specific example you're thinking of? Perhaps I could help you unravel this tapestry."

"No, no. It's nothing like that. I only wanted to know more about how it works."

"Well, there are others who would know more than I. You know that I've always been far more interested in sewing and saving." There was a certain degree of alliteration when she said it, but nothing like it is in English. "Why don't you try talking to your grandmother? You know she loves to see you."

Grandmother is an interesting laume. She resembles far more of the more scary stories I've heard of our kind. A crone rather than a bestial maiden. She's one of the greatest seers I've ever known, but she can be quite intense. It's almost like she can see right through you. It makes lying to her rather difficult. "I wouldn't want to bother her."

"Oh, I'm sure it won't be any bother at all."

"Mother—"

"This has been bothering you for far too long. If my words aren't enough to assuage your doubts, then perhaps someone else's can. Please, talk to your grandmother. She hasn't heard from you in months."

Slowly, reluctantly, I nod. "I will, Mother."

Pulling me into a hug, she rests her head on my shoulder. "There's my flower. Give her my love."

"I will," I say, wrapping my arms around her. I hope she won't expect me to bring a sacrifice.

❖

On the way—an hour out of the way—I find a friend of mine in her spring. Her nubile form lies supine atop a rock, the water gently sloshing around her. She loves claiming that she's responsible for the common tales of us bathing in springs, but unless she's the oldest laume I've ever met, I'm fairly certain she's full of shit.

"Good evening, Zuzane," I call.

She stirs from her perch, her head rising lazily. "Oh." She sits up, an amused look on her face. "Fancy seeing you here, Roze."

"Where else would I ever find you?"

"I've been known to visit a bathhouse in the nearby town. You're welcome to join me."

I roll my eye. I swear, some people. It's like they don't even know how to work.

"And you don't even know how to relax."

She can't read minds.

"Can so."

"You simply know me too well."

"Or I can see the future and know what you were going to say."

"I wasn't going to say it."

"Or were you?" She smirks.

Heaving out a sigh, I hike up my dress and stride across her lake. "I was not."

"This is a no-clothing-allowed area. How are we to lure wayward travelers off their path if we don't look enticing?" She lies back to show just how she intends to entice.

"Zu, please."

She pulls at my dress. "Why, do you have something to be ashamed of?"

"Zu, please," I repeat, firmer this time.

"You're no fun."

"I'm lots of fun."

Zuzane shakes her head. "When's the last time you even tried to relax? You used to play with me, go swimming, you know, have fun."

"There's no time."

Before I have a chance to even process what she's doing, she pushes me off the rock.

Fresh spring water fills my mouth. I splash, my dress soaked and clinging to me as I right myself, spitting out the fresh water. It actually tasted quite nice, but I'm not here for that. "Zuzane of Cekiske," I holler, stomping back to her, sending spray out around me. "I need to talk to you about something important."

"Is it destiny? And the immutability of fate? Because you talk about that all the time."

I falter, staring, the fight going out of me. I kick the water, sending a wave over her.

"Hey!" She jumps up, glaring.

I smirk.

Never one to back down from a challenge, she charges, hurtling water in my face. As I prepare my response, I catch a glimpse of the soaked bag in the water. Great. Well, I wanted Lithuanian copies anyway. I'm still pissed, though, so I dump an entire armful of water right on her head.

As we play, the sky darkens. I'm not sure if this counts as a storm dance or if it's merely chance, but we have to huddle in a nearby cave when lightning starts crashing down. At least it helps me unwind a little. But it means I'll have to wait to see my grandmother after all. I'll try not to be too bothered. I do love her. Genuinely. And she loves me. But talking to her about this is beyond terrifying. I can't let her know too much, and doing precisely that is the very purpose of her being.

Chapter Seven

Dovana

As soon as my class ends, I dash out the door. Taya's class doesn't let out for another half hour, so I'm not quite sure what I'm hurrying for, but I need to talk to her. I at least need to talk to someone, and I can't go home since Caroline is busy. I better remember to grab food for her, can't forget that. I'll invite Taya to get pizza; that'll make it easy.

I find a bench in the hall outside her classroom and pull the letter out of my backpack. I've made a good bit of progress, but this thing is not short.

I've told you about Zuzane before, right? She got her own spring last week. She had been vying for a bathhouse with another laume, Egle. I don't think I've ever mentioned her. We're not close. There's nothing against sharing, but you know those water laumes, they tend to be so territorial and competitive. But she's been excited. She actually threw a party, and that's not a thing we tend to do at all. There were all kinds of other beings there. My mother was intent on convincing me to start looking for a man to breed with.

Maybe I'm not ready for it.

But the party was a lot of fun. I'd never been to one before. Have you been going to a lot of parties at your school? I don't really know what they entail. I assume there's a lot of drinking. She had found some human liquor and brought it, and I simply do not see the appeal. But the aitvaras *that came seemed to have a taste for the stuff. I think I've mentioned how large they can be when they're not in a home. The little spark in your house was nothing compared to this fellow. He took up nearly the whole spring and turned it into a veritable hot spring.*

Try not to let any come to your parties. They hog all of the food.

I stare at the ceiling, shaking my head as I pinch the bridge of my nose. Sometimes, she does seem to treat me as a diary. But I can't complain. I love seeing this glimpse into this world, into her life. Any time I don't have one of these to read, I can't help but wonder what she's up to. Even if she's never going to be more than a pen pal, I care about her. She's my best friend.

And she's not even willing to see me.

Groaning, I toss my head back, smacking it into the concrete wall behind me.

Ow.

I hold my head, hoping that no one saw that. I must look dumb right now.

My phone buzzes in my pocket, and I flip it open. *Don't forget not to come home until six!* Thanks, Caroline. Way to make a girl feel wanted.

I type a quick response with the word function and let her know that I remembered. While I'm messaging people, I let Taya know that I'm waiting for her and ask if pizza is all right.

It takes a few minutes, but she says, *You're always waiting for me. I just assumed I'd see you. And pizza sounds wonderful.*

I call her a bitch and return to my letter.

It seems that she's been hanging out with Zuzane more than she used to. At least from what she says. I wonder if it's because she's not seeing her mother as often, so she's feeling lonelier. I know I went through that when I first ran off to college. Fortunately, I had a roommate to distract me.

Speaking of, her class files out. "Hey slut," the familiar accented voice calls from off to the side.

I just called her a bitch. What should I go with? "What's up, skank?"

She shakes her head. "You're hopeless."

"What?"

Chuckling, she gestures for us to walk. "Let's go grab some pizza."

I guess that'll give me time to sort out what I want to say. This is going to be complicated.

❖

Taya and I have to wait in a surprisingly long line. Apparently, 4:30 is a popular time for dinner. Who'd have guessed?

"How was class?" I try asking. Even as badly as I need to confide in her, I'd rather we hide away in an alcove and wait for our food first.

"Did you want me to talk about my physics course? 'Cause every time I've tried, you've zoned out within a few seconds."

"I have not."

"Equations."

I stare at the menu.

She chortles, shaking her head. I'm too far gone for her to even be offended. "Fine, then how was your class?"

"Oh, it was pretty great. We're still going over Kierkegaard's spheres of existence. It's honestly been really interesting having to reexamine how I feel about the religious sphere and—"

"Vana."

I give her a confused look. "What?"

"Who?"

"Soren Kierkegaard. He's one of my favorite philosophers. It's probably really between him and Hume. I've gone over him in class before, but that was when I first tried a philosophy course as a freshman, so it's nice getting to have a look at him now that I'm more mature and see how my beliefs have changed."

"Yeah, so mature."

"I am!"

Flashing a playful grin, she *tsks* at me. "What am I gonna do with you?"

"I think you've done enough."

The grin vanishes, her jaw dropping. "And what do you mean by that?"

"You know exactly what I mean," I say. I really do try not to hold a grudge. It's hard not to after what she pulled, but she's still my best friend. But sometimes our playing around does just remind me too much of how little she thinks of me.

"Oh, do I?"

"Yeah. Pretty sure you do."

"Ma'am," someone behind her says. Judging by the exasperated tone in their voice, possibly not for the first time. "Your order."

Taya turns, an apologetic look on her face, and orders a couple slices of margherita pizza.

I order a slice of veggie and one of whatever the specialty is before remembering to add Caroline's usual. Since she's paying me back, will have to wait either way, and will share it, I order a whole pizza for her. We head up the little set of stairs and find a spot to sit without too many people around.

"Please, no more philosopher lectures," Taya says, sipping her drink.

I forgot to get one. "Well, if I didn't have to go grab something, I would. You could use some Hume in your life." I know I still sound pissed, but I try to at least make it into a joke.

"What does that even mean?"

I ignore her and head off to order a diet soda.

Once I'm newly situated, I stare at my bag. What if she still doesn't believe me? And then I'll be stuck here with her until I can go home. Am I sure this is a good idea?

"Did you want to do anything this weekend? That movie I've been looking forward to just came out here if you're interested."

"I'm not watching anything in Russian."

"I watched that Lithuanian movie with you."

"Not the same." I sigh. If the alternative is fighting over Russia again, I may as well just put it out there. "Do you remember when we were roommates?"

"You mean when we were dating?"

Groaning, I nod. "Until you ruined everything."

"I wanted you to get help. You're the one who flipped out."

I turn on her, glaring, my hand still in my backpack. "I didn't need help."

"You were putting food outside our window, convinced a fairy was going to come take it. I thought you were on drugs."

How did I ever manage to forgive her in the first place? This was why we didn't talk about this shit. "I'm not crazy. Oh, for fuck's sake, just look for yourself." I pull the dozens of pages of the letter out of my bag and set them on the table. "This is from Roze. She sends them every year. I have more back home. I tried to tell you at the time, but you wouldn't have any of it."

"Roze is—"

"That 'fairy,' as you say."

She glances up, concern clear on her face. "Dovana—"

"Just look at it. You know full well I didn't write that whole thing."

"No, your hand writing is nowhere near this nice."

"My handwriting is fine. I won an award for calligraphy in middle school."

"I know your handwriting, and it's not like this. But that doesn't mean that it's some…what was the word?"

"Laume."

"It doesn't mean that a laume wrote it. You could have a pen pal." She never believes me. I should've known better than to try to talk to her about it again. I could have Roze herself with me, and it still wouldn't get through Taya's thick skull.

"I do have a pen pal. That doesn't make her human."

"Vana—"

"I know what I'm talking about. I'm not crazy."

She sighs, staring right into my eyes. I wish she didn't look so caring. It makes it harder to be mad at her. "These things aren't real."

"They are. I've seen her and others."

"And that's why you need help."

"I saw the counselor. She says I'm fine." I cross my arms. "Just read the fucking letter."

She starts to say something else when two metal plates with pizza slices are set in front of us. "Numbers forty-two and forty-three?" the server checks.

"Yeah," we both say.

She runs off, and Taya looks between the letter and her food. "I don't want to get food on it."

"Then don't. Just look, please. You're my best friend, and I need you to believe me."

She swallows, licking her lips as her eyes fail to meet mine. "How about I take this with me and have a look at it?"

"I haven't finished reading it."

That seems to give her pause. She looks between it and me. "You—"

"I didn't write it."

"I know."

"I leave her food and a letter in my window every year on the anniversary of the day we met, when she helped me find my way home. And every single time, there's one of these letters waiting. It happened in Babtai, it happened once we moved to Toronto, and it's happened at each of my dorms. Roze is real, Taya. And she's my friend. As my friend, that should mean something to you."

"It does," she says.

"Then stop acting like I'm crazy."

"Why are you showing me this now? It's been two years since I confronted you about this."

I shrug. "I thought I shouldn't tell anyone, but now I'm tired of having to treat it like a secret. I'm tired of her treating me like a secret." I take a deep breath. This was the part I really wanted to talk to her about, but I needed her to believe me first. "In the letter"—I gesture about halfway down the first page—"she mentions that she's gone to visit other people after she rescued them, but she's never done so with me. We're friends. We talk every year. And I don't understand why she wouldn't. And I wanted to talk to someone about it, and I thought if anyone would listen to me…" I let out an exasperated sigh. "I should've just called my mother."

"Well, it couldn't just mean that she's not…wait, your mother knows?"

I blink. "Yes? Why wouldn't she?"

"But…how?"

"She was there. And she and my father used the gold that Roze gave us to move out here."

"She gives you gold?"

I nod.

Her mouth opens and closes a few times. "Why didn't you lead with that?"

"Well, I actually have a reason to keep that secret. People steal gold. I trust you a lot, but that doesn't mean I want you to know how much money I have." How on earth do I still trust her? I know I'm not lying when I say it, but she doesn't deserve it. She could just believe me for once in her damn life. Why would I lie about this?

"Show me a piece, then. Between that and the letter"—she sighs—"maybe I could at least be open to the possibility."

I blink. She's actually considering it? It's still not enough. "Can't you just believe me because I know what I'm talking about?"

"It's not that simple."

I nod. "It is. Taya, you're my friend. This is important to me. Believe me. I don't care how much it shatters your worldview, it's true. And I need to talk to you about it."

She lets out a low groan and slides the letter back across the table. "Fine, I'll accept it at face value for now. Tell me about it while I eat, and I'll do what I can. But I want more evidence later."

Considering this, I chew on my lip. It's a fairer compromise than I should have expected. "All right. But you have to actually be willing to accept what I give you."

She holds out her hands. "I'll do what I can."

"Okay."

She chews while I go over everything from the beginning again, like I tried to last time when she wasn't ready to listen. By the time I get to the present, she's finished both her slices, and I've barely eaten half of one. I decide to busy myself with that while she mulls my words over.

"So you think she's avoiding you?"

"I don't know." I suck on my teeth and move my mouth around to try to dislodge a stubborn piece of cheese, and she's kind enough to look away.

"Maybe there's something she's not telling you? If we're going to assume that it's not just a trick or that your mom isn't writing the letters."

"Taya!" She managed what, a full minute of an open mind before she went right back to assuming I'm crazy, lying, a moron, or all three?

"I know, I know."

"And my mom definitely can't scale the side of my dorm building," I snap

She hesitates. "Yeah, she is a little on the heavy side."

I roll my eyes. "Why do I even talk to you?"

"Because you love me."

It's true, but right now it hardly feels like enough of a reason. "Besides that."

She smirks.

I chew on my second slice. It's spicier than expected. I'm not quite sure what all they put on it. I try taking smaller bites and washing it down. "Maybe there's something she's scared of? It could be my parents? Or maybe she thinks she's not allowed to since her mother wouldn't let her? I don't know that her mother wouldn't let her, but she was six when we first met."

"Wait, she's the same age as you? Aren't fairies not able to have kids?"

I shrug. "From what I've seen when I looked up myths, they can't, but I'm not sure how it works. And people could just get stuff wrong."

"All right. Not that important. So what do you think then?"

I blow out a breath. I wish I knew. "Maybe I should try inviting her?"

"How're you going to do that if she only comes once a year?"

"Well, I could try what I normally do. I never really bothered leaving a gift for her on any other day. It could be that she can come any time."

She shrugs. "Can I join you? I'd really like to see the evidence here."

"She might not come if you're there. Hell, maybe the reason she never comes is because I've always had a roommate or my parents." Could that really be it? Has she been avoiding me this whole time just because I didn't pay a bit extra to not have a roommate? If she'd just told me, I'd have done it in an instant. Not like that means much when she gives me the money in the first place. I start to run my fingers through my hair, stopping to wipe them on a napkin when I think better of it. "Not that that seems to stop her with others."

"Let me be there for you," she insists, her voice firm. "If what you say is…no, I've been a shitty friend over this, and it already took so much from us. Let me go with you, and if she doesn't show up, I won't say I told you so or anything because it's not the day she visits you on, so it doesn't say anything for sure."

I take the time to finish my pizza before responding. I guess I'm giving her a second chance with all this. Maybe this time, I won't have to see a therapist. "Promise you won't be a bitch about it?"

"Scout's honor."

"I am two-thousand-percent sure you were never a Boy Scout."

"There are scouts in Russia."

"Were you one?"

She tilts her head. "Well, no. But I promise."

"Fine. But I'm not gonna be your friend anymore if you break it."

Her gaze falls back to the table, and her fingers dance on it for a moment. "I won't. I know this is important to you. Will Caroline mind my coming?"

"No, she owes me. And said you could."

"I think the second part may be more important."

"Maybe." I shrug. "Well, we still have to wait on her pizza. But want to pick up something at the movie kiosk? We could steal her pizza and watch a rom-com."

"God, how are you such a straight girl?"

"You're one to talk."

"At least I actually dated a girl in the last year."

I glare at her. "Why am I inviting you over again?"

By way of apology, she gives me an affable grin. "We've been over this. But fine, rom-com, pizza, and beer sounds great."

"I didn't say beer."

"It was implied."

We get vodka on the way home instead. I suppose if she's going to humor me, I might as well humor her for being a damn Russian. Or maybe I just wanted vodka to drown myself in when Roze doesn't show.

CHAPTER EIGHT

ROZE

Even as a laume travels, my grandmother's home is a long trek. It takes me hours to find her secluded little abode: a damp, dark cave affixed with all sorts of magical accoutrements. I've never been quite certain if she keeps them because she actually uses them or because they add the appearance she wants for when humans see it.

About halfway in, I find her, ever the picture of an old hag, stirring some sort of cauldron. I wonder what's in it. "Roze, is that you?" she asks without turning.

I stop a few meters away, not sure what to say. I need her advice. Badly. But I can't risk giving everything away. "Yes, Grandmother."

She turns, a warm smile on her face as she beckons. She's more hunched than I recall, but she always looked aged, even when I was a newborn. "Come in, come in. I've nearly finished fixing stew. Are you hungry?"

"It was a long walk. I would appreciate it."

"Sit, sit." She clears beakers, a mortar and pestle, and pages of notes from a table, and pulls out an old chair, the once-black paint showing the wood beneath it.

I do as she tells me. "Thank you."

The stirring resumes, and she seems to lose track of time, not bothering to say any more. I'm not sure if I should ask her something. She's much more insightful than me. I'd rather not risk her finding out what I want to avoid.

"That should do it." She shakes a large canister of salt over the pot and scoops out the contents with two healthy-sized bowls. "Now, where am I going to sit?" she ponders.

I start to stand.

"Don't you dare. You've been walking all day, relax." She waddles off and returns a few minutes later holding a stool, again waving me off when I try to help her as she sets it before the table and moves more of her equipment. "Now, where were we? I believe you wanted my advice. Something to do with the future?"

"We haven't had that part of the conversation yet, Grandmother," I mutter. She always gets so confused. Sometimes I fear that I'll be like that too if I give in to my powers the same way she has.

"Ah, right." She raises the stew to her lips, taking a deep sip of hot broth. "Ah, perfect. Is it not to your liking?"

I take a sip and end up draining half the bowl before I'm finished. Wow, I was hungrier than expected. "No, it's great."

"I'm glad to hear that. So you just got here?"

"Yes."

"Then I ask what it is that you want, and you tell me that your mother told you to come here."

"Traditionally, I would supply my own response."

She chuckles, swirling her stew. "Oh, but there's no meat on your bones. Let me get you some food."

"You already did."

She glances at my stew. "More then." She approaches the untended cauldron with my bowl and tops it off before setting it back on the table. "Much better."

"Thank you, Grandmother."

"Hello, Roze. It's good to see you. Your mother must have sent you."

I nod. "It's nice to see you as well."

"But that doesn't mean that it won't work."

"What?"

She shakes her head. "I haven't offered the first suggestion yet, have I? You said you were trying to change the future? What have you seen that so troubles you?"

Has she already seen my answer? Of course I wouldn't tell her, not yet anyway. She'd have to have seen it from some far-off future when it's no longer relevant, and she doesn't like to skip that far ahead if she can avoid it. "It's nothing like that. My interest is purely theoretical."

"Now that's never true. What's the worry?"

Well, she'll likely forget that I didn't answer if I just press on. "There's a future that I've been trying to alter for over a decade. No matter what I do, the end result is the same, and I've merely delayed it. Can fate really be immutable? If anyone would know how to change a destiny that stubborn, it would be you, right, Grandmother?"

She sips her stew as she considers. Or possibly considers calling out my avoiding her question. "Some futures are not so malleable."

"Like death? Or love?"

"Or even some bad stew. It's not about the importance of the event. It's about the likelihood of it. Everyone will die, most people will find love, and everyone will eat bad stew."

"Right," I agree hesitantly.

She finishes and lets the empty bowl fall to the floor. Maybe she thought she'd already put it away. "Say for instance, that your dear friend was in an abusive relationship. You may have seen a future where he killed her. Or perhaps a she rather than a he. Humans tend to those odd choices as much as they tend toward killing. It's best not to judge them."

"I think we can judge in that situation."

"For the murder perhaps. But not for going back to her. No matter how you tried to change the future, there's nothing that can guarantee that she'll free herself. The best you can do is offer a supportive environment, but until she decides that she's willing to move on, not even the gods themselves could tell her otherwise."

"I'm not sure I understand. No one is in an abusive relationship."

"The stew, then. You can tell her that she won't like it, but until she tastes it, it won't change a thing. Even if you were to take all of her ingredients and pots, that would only delay it. Someday, she'll eat that terrible stew you so fear. Not even your sight can prevent that, my dear child."

I sigh. Did that answer my question? I'm not sure. But I really want more stew now. With honey bread. Or just the honey bread. "Thank you," I try.

"Now, what was it that you wanted to tell me?"

"I already did, Grandmother."

She pauses, staring, her milky eyes seeming to burn with an ineffable insight. "No, you didn't. What is it that you want to change, my dear? I can keep a secret. With my help, we may be able to find the one way to change that poor dear's future."

"It's nothing like that," I insist, harsher than I mean.

"Roze—"

"No, thank you for the help. I was just wondering about the principles behind our abilities. That's all." I stand, taking a deep breath. "You've helped me enough."

"No one worries themselves over theory. Not even as gifted a student as you."

If I was so gifted a student, I would already know all of this. I'd have learned everything I could from my grandmother years ago.

But I can't study under her. It's always been too great a risk. She could find the same future I've seen and know exactly what I'm trying to change, and my family can never learn that. They wouldn't understand. "I really must be off," I say. "I'm sure a child will need me soon."

"I don't see you rescuing anyone soon."

I grind my teeth, staring at her. "Still, I should be where I can more easily travel."

"Roze—"

With a deep breath, I take her hands. "Thank you, Grandmother. I'll think about what you said, and maybe we can work on it more later. But for now, I really need to go." This was too risky. If she hadn't been so disordered, she'd have known exactly what I saw. What little answer she gave wasn't worth it.

She nods, not quite meeting my eyes. "Very well, flower. I'll see you when you're ready. Take care of yourself and the girl until then."

She's already learned too much. I give her a quick peck on the cheek and head out, looking for anyone who may be in need of my help. I need to focus on anything other than my own life.

CHAPTER NINE

DOVANA

Someone shaking my shoulders stirs me from...crap, did I fall asleep? I look up to see Taya staring slack-jawed at the window as Caroline's sleepy breathing comes from the other bed.

I look at the windowsill. The hunk of honey wheat bread I left out is floating.

I blink.

It's still floating.

As I lean closer, I can see little wings flapping away to support their bearer and the bread at least twice their size. Some short, messy hair pokes out just over the crust, and as I adjust my view, I can see closed eyes as the sprite eagerly chews.

The bed creaks when I inch closer, but apparently, the fae really love honey wheat, as it doesn't seem to notice. When I'm close enough, I lean toward the open window, and as quickly as I can manage, snatch the figure out of the air, bread and all.

It squeaks in protest, the noise muffled by my hand and the food. I slam the window shut with my other hand.

Caroline jolts awake at the sound. "What? What happened? Vana?"

I swallow, taking in a deep breath to steady my nerves. No one else has ever seen anything like this around me. Roze vanished, and she's never shown her face again. My parents had been aware of the aitvaras, but I was the only one to ever see the little flaming chicken myself.

My whole life—though I never gave into the fears—part of me has been scared that I was simply crazy. I had the gold, I had proof, my parents believed me, so the fear never grew too strong. But especially after Taya made me see that therapist, it's always eaten away at me. What if I am schizophrenic? If the gold came from…okay, the crazy theory doesn't make much sense. But it still eats at me sometimes.

So holding definitive proof, I can barely breathe as I unveil the little thing.

The second my hand opens, it darts around, heading toward the window, then back to the bread, then the ceiling, back to the bread, then toward the door, only to yo-yo again. "Unhand me," it shouts as it stands on the bread in my palm.

"I'm not holding you."

"What the fuck is that?" Caroline screams. "I'm still dreaming. That has to be it. Is that insect talking?"

"Put your glasses on," I insist.

Taya inhales sharply. "There's no way—"

"What the fuck?" Caroline repeats.

The sprite darts off, falling right back to the bread and taking another bite.

"It's a little fairy," Caroline breathes.

"What did you say?" he shouts, his naked glittery body flapping into her face.

"Get off me!"

"Why, I'll—"

"Aren't you supposed to be nice?"

It punches her. There's a slight indent on her cheek, but it fills right back out, and she seems more surprised than hurt. "Am not a bloody fairy!" Despite the squeak of the voice, he sounds decidedly masculine. That hypothesis seems rather firmly confirmed by exactly what else is flapping in her face.

"They don't like that word," I say, sighing. This isn't at all what I was hoping for. I guess it'll convince Taya I'm not crazy, but I wanted to see Roze.

"That's not Roze, right?" Taya asks. "Like, you said she was human-sized. And only had one eye. And was a girl. And didn't have wings."

"What the hell are you lot on about?" he asks, flying at us only to land on the bread again and start eating.

Caroline looks between the three of us, apparently upset that we're not as shocked as she is. "How is there a fairy here?"

"What did I say?" He punches her chin harder this time, enough that she moves…very slightly.

"But aren't you—"

"Caroline," I insist. "Try fair one."

"At least this *feek* has some bloody manners," he says. "Not that it stopped her from snatching me away in the middle of my sodding snack. Nonetheless, she gave me some bread first, so it's not too rotten, but this *mog* acting the maggot—" He shakes his head.

I try very hard not to laugh. Curse words in a voice that sounds like Mickey Mouse inhaled some helium may be one of the funniest things I've ever heard. I don't succeed.

"And what's the gas?" He turns to me. "Some scatter of *bures* tempts me with a smidgen of bread, only to drag me into…what is this, a slumber party? Am I to tell you all some scary stories while you practice scoring each other?"

Caroline stares at the little thing. "What did any of that mean?"

"I don't think he likes you," Taya said.

"So this yoke does have a voice."

"I've talked already," she insists.

"Hardly." He picks up a big piece of the bread, stuffing it into his mouth and chewing as he looks around the room. "So what do you want? Is this some sort of sex thing? 'Cause I'm always ready for a bit o' *craic*."

"Can we just put him back outside?" Taya asks.

I groan. I wish we could. "I have some questions."

"There any bread in it for me?"

I glance toward the rest of the loaf sitting on top of my microwave, well, Caroline's microwave. "All right. *After* you answer."

"Then let me finish this one first at least. Have some manners, for God's sake." He makes good on his word, stuffing nearly the entire piece into his mouth, chewing it in a scant few bites, only to swallow it and stay as small and slim as before. "So what did you bloody *bures* want to know?"

I've known Irish people. They don't talk like this. What is wrong with this thing? And more importantly, what do I want to know? I didn't have any plans. I just assumed that Roze would come, or she wouldn't, but I can't pass up this chance. "I don't suppose you know a laume named Roze?"

"'Fraid not, *feek*. Only known one laume in all my years, and she was a right muppet."

"Well, is there any way I could contact her?"

"Have you tried a phone?"

I roll my eyes. "That's not helpful. If you want the bread—"

"All right, all right. I assume you know where all the fiends in town like to congregate?"

I stare at him, blinking a few times as I look for any response. "I'm sorry?"

"Shite, if you don't even know that, then how'd you end up with me? Don't answer that. If I tell you where to find her, or at least someone who might know her, then I can have the bread and leave?"

I nod. "For that, you can take the bread and freely leave." I've talked to Roze enough—and read a few books on the subject—to know how to respectfully talk to the fae.

"Right, right. Well, there's this community center, as they call it. I don't know how to tell you where it is, but it's a little round building, and at nights, there's always a full-blown bazaar in it." He points one of his little fingers toward the corner. "It's a short flight that way. Just go there, and I'm sure you'll find it."

"I need more than that."

"I gave you what I can. Now keep up your end, you gobshite."

Pushing it any further is unlikely to help. It's something to go on, at least. I grab the loaf from the microwave and hand him the whole thing. To my surprise, he easily picks up a package of bread four times his size and flies to the window. I open it for him, and he flies off, flipping us off on his way.

"What the fuck?" Caroline repeats.

Taya and I look between each other. I've avoided telling people for so long, but it's too late for that now. I tell her the whole story only to receive yet another, "What the fuck?"

"Sorry," I mutter.

"Fairies are real?"

Taya says, "Probably shouldn't say that word."

"Right." She nods.

I sigh, leaning back in my bed. "I didn't think I'd ever have a reason to tell you all of this." Especially not after how Taya had reacted. But now even she believes me. I knew I wasn't crazy, but at the same time, it's hard not to be relieved by being so solidly vindicated.

"But it's real." She clutches her blanket, staring at the window the little fair one had flown off through half an hour ago.

"It is. All of it is real."

"And you're trying to find one? That Roze."

"Just go back to sleep, Caroline. It's late."

"I was punched by a fai—fair one."

"Did it hurt?" Taya asks.

She shakes her head. "No."

"Then don't worry."

"I—I…" She touches her cheek and chin where it hit her.

"So, you believe me now?" I ask Taya.

She shrugs. "Kind of hard not to at this point. I'm sorry, Vana."

"It's okay."

"No, it's not. You were my girlfriend, and I should have believed you."

I turn away, studying the wall firmly. For months, I wanted her to say something like that, but I've moved past it, and now it's just strange to hear. It honestly hurts more than it feels good. It's too little too late. Not for our friendship, but for that to have really meant anything as a partner. "Don't worry about it."

"Then let me help."

I stare at her, scarcely willing to believe I heard her right. "What?"

"You're trying to find Roze. Let me help you. The directions that thing gave us are really vague. If we work together, it should be a lot easier. We can find it, Vana. We can find that community center."

To my surprise, my eyes start watering, and I throw my arms around her. I really hadn't wanted to do this alone. "Thank you," I whisper, any thought of sleep vanishing. I got enough. Probably. Like, at least two hours. "Can we go now?"

Her expression turns from comforting to surprised to mirthful, and she chuckles. "Yeah. Not like I'm getting back to sleep after that."

Caroline stares at us. "You're going to leave me here?"

"In our dorm room?"

"But...but..."

"Do you want to go look for fiends?"

She hesitates, looking between us and her pillow. "Let me get ready first. I'll probably have to hurry back for class."

CHAPTER TEN

ROZE

I feel the call. There's a child in danger. And I'm already well away from my grandmother, so it's not simply an excuse to not talk about my issues.

The forest moves around me, shifting from one country to another. I raise my foot in Lithuania, set it down in Latvia, raise the other, and set it down in Turkey. Soon, I'm in the humid rain forests of Brazil. The wails of a child fill the air as two other laumes stand before her. One is crouching, but the other seems to be her size. Their goat-legs seem to scare the little girl as much as her present predicament.

I know the older laume, Ruta, but I'm not familiar with the younger one. "Yours, I assume?" I ask. Normally, I'd be informed, at least I'd think I would. A laume managing to produce an offspring is an occasion worth celebrating. It's rare and vital. How did I not know?

She glances to me, looking confused for a moment before her gaze falls on the young laume. "Yes. Say hello, Smilte."

The girl waves at me before turning back to the human. "It's okay," she insists. She can't be more than a year older than the frightened baby. Now if only she spoke Spanish. Or is it Portuguese? We rarely go this far. They have their own spirits here; things must have been desperate for all three of us to be summoned.

"It's a pleasure to meet you, Smilte. What a lovely name." I glance around, looking for any reason that the child would be so upset.

She nods, her eyes staying on the child. She'll grow up to be a natural-born rescuer. Good. We can always use more.

The child asks something in a language I don't know. I assume Portuguese. I feel like I heard that is what they speak here. It sounds a little different from Spanish, but that could be my imagination. Hell, she could be speaking Italian, and I still wouldn't know. I only even learned English because of Dovana.

Smilte holds out her hand, trying to look as calm as can be.

Something smells.

The girl stares at the hand.

Like barbecue. Hickory smoke…or not quite that.

"Please," Smilte insists.

"Child," Ruta says, her voice calm and soothing. "Come with us. We will take you to safety."

She seems to relax a little, but she still doesn't take the hand. She stares at the two pairs of cloven feet before looking me straight in the eye and withdrawing, pulling away from us. She doesn't run, but she steps back a few feet.

It's not just the smell. The air seems to be thicker than usual. And I hear…oh Vaiva. I turn around, gazing as far off as I can. There's the faintest hint of smoke through the trees. It's not near, and it doesn't seem to be coming fast, but if we don't get this child out of here, she will end up burning. No wonder this felt so important. She's not just lost; she could die. "There's a fire," I say, trying not to let the fear creep into my voice.

"I know," Ruta says.

Smilte, however, doesn't seem to have realized. She looks between the two of us, shock clear on her face. "What? But we have to get her out of here. How can there be a fire?"

"Let's pick her up."

"Yes, because foreign, devil-looking figures picking her up near a forest fire isn't going to traumatize her," Ruta snaps back.

"It's better than her dying."

She groans, causing the child to only retreat farther.

Smilte takes a few steps toward her, and she doesn't retreat. She points to herself, "Smilte."

The child gawks.

She gestures again, more dramatically this time, before repeating "Smilte."

The child says something that includes Smilte in it. Presumably asking if it's her name, but she could also be asking what it means.

The little laume nods. "Yes, that's me. And you are?" She gestures toward her with an open hand.

She looks between us again before whispering, "Aline."

"Hi, Aline," Smilte says, her tone overly friendly. "It's great to meet you. We need to go."

Confusion retakes Aline's features.

"Aline," I try. "Look." I point to the smoke. "We want to bring you back home. We know where your family is." I know she'll be okay. We're here, and we would never allow any ill fate to befall a child in our care. It's so wonderful to know I can actually accomplish a goal. To know that no matter how dire the circumstances, I don't need to worry. I just wish it was true outside of my duties.

She stares at me.

"Please," Ruta says, her voice breaking.

Smilte holds out her hand again, gesturing away from the fire. "Home? Mama?"

I'm not sure if Aline understands either of the words or decides that it's worth trusting the other child, but she takes her hand. Smilte really is going to be something special.

We lead Aline away. We can't travel with her, so it takes the better part of three hours to arrive at her home. Smilte doesn't let go of her hand even once during the entire journey.

Watching her, I can't help but think of when I was in her shoes. My first time saving someone. The day I met Dovana. My heart sinks. I try so hard to ignore her, to prevent what has to happen, but I just always come back to her. So much for my distraction.

Aline's parents squeal when they see her, paying Smilte no mind. Perhaps goat legs are normal here. Ruta and I watch from the shadows as Smilte gets to see what our job entails. Seeing that reunion can be one of the most rewarding experiences there is.

After minutes of hugging and exclaiming, the mother finally seems to notice Smilte. She says something, and Smilte naturally doesn't reply. To my astonishment, rather than running away, the humans keep talking, and Smilte ends up going inside, presumably for food. She's more than earned it.

I turn to Ruta and finally ask the question that's been nagging at me. "How didn't I know?"

She takes in a deep breath, turning to face me. Her expression grows forlorn until tears shine in her eyes, and she has to take another breath. "I didn't think I'd have her to share."

I shake my head. "I don't understand."

Her exhalation is shaky, and her dress bunches in her fist. "I only recently got her back."

"From whom?"

She nods, blinking away those tears. "Her father. I'd told him before that my people would need her, that this is how it works, but as soon as she was born…" Tears fall anew as she starts sobbing, struggling to even force out the words. "He…he…" She chokes, snorting as she tries to collect her breath.

"It's okay." I place a hand on her shoulder.

She takes a few more breaths before finally meeting my eye again. I move my hand down to hers, giving it a reassuring squeeze.

"Take all the time you need." What could he have done? Did he really take her? No wonder she'd want to keep it quiet. She lost a child laume. We need everyone we can get. We might've been able to help get Smilte back, but I can't blame her for not wanting to face the shame that would bring.

"He ran off with her," she finally says, her hoarse voice scarcely more than a whisper. "I've been looking for her this whole time. His family wouldn't even talk to me anymore."

"I'm so sorry."

She holds my hand, squeezing a bit tighter than is comfortable, but if it helps, it helps. "I couldn't tell all of you. I couldn't bring myself to talk about it. It was my job to bring a new girl into our family, and instead, I lost her. And I thought I'd never see her again."

"We would've helped you, Ruta. You know that."

She shakes her head again. "No, you know how it would've been received. I had failed. I lost her. If I hadn't managed to…" Another shake and more sobs.

"You have her now. And she seems far better adapted than I would have feared. When did you finally get her back?"

"A few months ago." The words fall from her lips as if she can no longer keep them in. "I was terrified. It was days before she was even willing to face me. She wanted to go back to her father, but if I let her see him, I'd have never gotten her back."

"Well, it seems she's doing better now."

Ruta nods. "I started letting her watch me at work, helping out a little and telling her more about what she'd grow to do. She took to it so naturally, Roze. Even more than you did. Much more than I ever did. You saw her."

"I did. She gained the child's trust like it was nothing. I can scarcely believe she was denied a proper upbringing." My mother always acted like I was a natural. If that's the case, then Smilte is a prodigy. "What was her father?"

She bites her lip. "You'll think less of me."

"Nothing could shake my view of you, dearest Ruta."

She seems to fall back in on herself, clutching her head in her hands as she admits, "Baubas."

I swallow, blinking. "I'm sorry?" I couldn't have heard her right. No one could breed with that thing. Even for monsters, it's a monster. He'd sooner eat a child than raise it.

"Well, I couldn't find anyone more reasonable," she insists. "It's not like I was seeking him out."

"How did that even happen?" And why would he possibly wind up with a laume? What would he have wanted with poor Smilte?

A low whimper echoes between her fingers. "Roze—"

"I still don't judge you." I wrap my arms around her, hugging her tightly. "It's okay. I can certainly understand how she was hard to find. I didn't even know he had family."

She nods against me.

"She must have been so horrified. I'm sorry."

A muffled sob sounds from under my chin.

"You did nothing wrong. You brought a wonderful child into our family and have made sure we can continue our duties." Now, if only I could do the same. "And you even managed to get her back when she was taken by"—I gulp—"him."

Pulling away, she looks up into my eye. "You really don't think I did anything wrong? I swear, it seemed like he was better than all the stories made him seem."

"I can't judge you. I wasn't there. I don't know what he may have done to woo you or how desperate things may have seemed. All I know is that it brought us Smilte, and that's wonderful."

Tears fall, but she doesn't look away or coil up again. "Thank you."

The door of the little cottage opens, and the human child hugs Smilte before finally letting her leave. She skips over to us, as happy as can be. Perhaps she was spared any horror stories of humans; it seems unlikely that Baubas would have cared to share them. "Hi, Mama," she says. "That was so much fun. You were right. This is much better than scaring them." I'm sorry, what? "I really like being a laume."

Ruta chews her lip again, offering a pained smile. "That's wonderful to hear, dear."

"Can we go save another one? There has to be one lost somewhere, right? I wanna try it again. This was great. I'm gonna be the best laume ever," she shouts.

"We'll know when it's time."

"But I wanna go now." She stomps her foot in the grass.

"I'm sure it will come soon."

She pouts, huffing and crossing her arms.

"This is what my first time was like as well," I say. "I knew right away that it was for me."

"Really?" she asks, seeming to forget that she's upset.

"I even made a friend who I'm still in touch with. Did you two manage to sort out a way to talk?"

She shakes her head. "No. I just ate their food while they said things I didn't understand."

"Perhaps the next one," I offer.

"You think so?" She sounds so worried. This must feel like the most important thing she's ever done or to ever happen to her.

"I know so." Befriending people you rescue is easy. And with luck, they won't have any wretched fates she'll have to avoid.

She grins, her teeth showing, any signs of distress having completely vanished. "Let's go then, Mama. We have to save someone."

"We will," Ruta says. "You'll know when it's time. Don't you want to properly meet your Aunt Roze first?"

"No." She shakes her head.

I chuckle. "I know how exciting it can be. But it'll come soon."

"But I want to now."

Before either of us can teach her the ever-important lesson of patience, we all feel it again. Back home. It must be Smilte's lucky day.

We head off, finding a lost child only for Smilte to befriend him as easily as the last one. We're lucky to have her. And I'm glad to see that my promise is coming true. I can already see a future with them forming a friendship that will guide them for the rest of their lives. When I'd promised her this future, I hadn't yet seen it, and yet I was dead on.

Now if only my own future ever gave me as much luck. After everything I've been told, I seem to still be at square one. Perhaps it truly is impossible.

Chapter Eleven

Dovana

Outside, we walk around the building as we try to orient ourselves to the exact direction the fair one had been pointing. It takes us about five minutes under the window, and we all end up pointing in different directions and rehashing the way he'd moved. Finally, we head northward, walking since the buses haven't started up yet.

"I can't believe we're doing this," Caroline mutters.

"What's not to believe?" Taya asks. "A fairy popped in through our window, and now we're off running around town in the middle of the night, trying to find a place where a bunch of monsters hang out. Seems like a pretty normal Thursday night to me."

Caroline sighs. "So it was really…I mean that was—"

"Don't call them fairies," I say, waving for them to hurry up. We need to hurry back before it gets too late, and I want to actually find the place first.

"But that is what he was, right?" Caroline asks. "I'm not going crazy? This is really…" She adjusts her glasses, taking in a deep breath as she stares at me, her jaw slack. "This is real?"

I nod, doing my best not to look too thrilled. This is going much better than when I tried to tell Taya. "Yes, it's real. Monsters are real. Hell, the fair one I'm looking for paid my tuition."

"What?" Her voice is flat, and she sounds more pissed than confused at this point. "So, what, you just found some bitch with wings to take care of everything for you? Do you know how expensive this place is? And you happen to have, what, a fairy sugar momma?"

My cheeks warm. "It's not like that. And I said not to call her a fairy. But she's not my sugar mommy. She's an old friend. And we haven't…no, that'd be weird. She gives me money because I give her bread."

"Can't she just buy bread?"

I shrug. I've always wondered about that. "They give money to the people they look after. I'm just blessed that she found me in the woods all those years ago."

"What do you mean she found you?"

With a heavy sigh, I tell the whole story, managing to only do a slightly passive-aggressive jab at Taya in the process, and explain how I met Roze as a child. When I finish, not only does my roommate look slack-jawed, but my best friend does as well. I'd just told her yesterday, hadn't I? "Is it really that strange?" I ask.

"Is it strange to have a magical best friend who gives you money every year?" Taya asks. "Yeah, a little."

"You're my best friend," I mutter.

"Well, I'm not paying your tuition."

"Why didn't you ever tell," Caroline begins. "Well, no, I guess that makes sense. But still, I mean, how would you have kept this a secret? You said she left gold here the other day? Wouldn't I have noticed that? Like if some strange fair…fair woman showed up at the window, watching us and leaving packages, shouldn't I have been able to tell? That was part of how I knew Santa wasn't real. I'd hear him if he was actually on the roof. Wait, is Santa real?"

I purse my lips, wanting to hold in the truth. I got made fun of the entirety of sixth and seventh grade for this, until I started lying about it. But she deserves an answer. "Yes."

"What?" Her jaw drops all the farther.

Taya blinks. "I'm sorry?"

"He's not like you think. And I don't have that much info on him, but Roze has met him. I asked her about him when I was a kid after I caught my parents leaving presents instead."

"Wow." Caroline shakes her head, staring at the ground. "I can't even imagine what that must have been like. You had this person who could give you a knowing answer to any crazy supernatural question you had. I had my pastor growing up, but she never really seemed like she knew, not really. But you had someone who has seen all of it, and it was completely normal for you. Even if she wasn't paying for your schooling, I'd still be jealous."

I shrug, turning away and looking at the road and our surroundings. It's nice not having to do this alone. I'd never had the courage to look for her before. Not since I was eight and tried to intentionally get lost in the woods.

We're about a kilometer from the school already, but with how fast he flew, that doesn't necessarily mean we're there. At least, I wouldn't think so. "How fast did he fly?"

"How the hell should I know?" Taya asks. Lacing her hands behind her head, she chuckles. "Oh, hey, I didn't realize this was where that pub was." She points at an old building on the right. "This was my favorite place freshman year."

I laugh. "I know. I was there."

"Oh. Right."

"Maybe, like, I don't know, ten kilometers an hour?" Caroline suggests, actually answering my question, unlike some people. "But he also kind of seemed like an idiot."

"Well, yeah. I'm not sure what that has to do with it, though."

"We're going off his vague directions when he very well could have no idea what he's talking about."

Chewing my lip, I meet her eyes, doing my best not to show my own doubts. "I don't have anything else to go on, Caroline. And I can't not do this. I need to talk to Roze. She's…she's my…" I groan. I wish I could even articulate why it's so important that I see her. "She's my friend. And it's been so long. And now that I know that I can actually talk to her, that I can see her in person again rather than having to count the days until her next letter…" I blink away tears. "I need this. I need to talk to her. I need to ask her why she never visited, but more importantly, I need to actually see her again. I know this is crazy, and I know that we have next to nothing to go off of, but we have this, and I have to try. And your coming with me means the world."

With a heavy sigh, Caroline nods. "I'm already here, Vana. I'm helping you. I'm just frustrated and confused."

"Me too."

"We should start a club," Taya chimes in.

"Maybe we should try asking people?"

"It's like four a.m. Who would we ask?" Even the pub is closed. The street is quiet and dark. I have absolutely no idea what to do.

Taya says, "Then let's split up."

"Why?"

"We need to cover more ground. We'll look around. It has to be somewhere within the next couple kilometers."

"And what if we find the place?" Caroline asks.

"Then we'll call each other."

"And be stuck waiting there alone with monsters? They could see us. Or eat us!"

She shrugs. "Then don't get eaten?"

"Maybe we should stay together," I suggest.

"It's like looking for a needle in a haystack," Taya says. "We'll never find it if we're all searching the same place. We don't have to get too far from each other, but we still need to actually all look. We'll call if we find anything or if we're in trouble."

"Fine, but if I'm robbed or eaten by monsters, it's your fault," Caroline says.

"I'll say as much at your funeral," Taya promises.

She rolls her eyes. "I appreciate that."

"So let's look," I say. And as we split up, I soon find how much quieter the street is when I'm on it alone. A chill runs up my spine, but I ignore it. I have to find her.

❖

Taya and Caroline run on ahead, the latter glancing around worriedly as she moves. The sun still hasn't risen, and we're not in the best part of town, but I'm sure we'll be fine. How much crime can there be where monsters hang out? Assuming we're in the right place and the monsters aren't the criminals.

I look every which way, desperate for any sign of something otherworldly. I wish I'd caught the name of that fair one. Maybe he'd answer to it, and I could ask him for more specifics or at least if I'm in the right place.

I swear I see something with horns run past the other end of an alley, but when I run through it, my foot sticking in things I'd really rather not think about, and make it out the other side, the road is as empty as the one I came from. There's not even the sound of footsteps. How crazy must I be to run toward some horned monster rather than away from it? Why am I so desperate to see her? Am I really not terrified? No, I am. I'm just angry. She's avoided me all this time when she didn't have to, and I want an explanation.

Heading up the block, hoping maybe I'll catch another glimpse of the creature, I find myself in a playground, the contorted structures of metal and plastic looking far more sinister in the dark. The wind blows, and the aching creak of chains fills the night. I spin in a circle, almost overjoyed at the idea that it could be a ghost—do ghosts even count as monsters—but it's just the swings. Sighing, I walk around the closed sign to sit down in one, silencing its scream.

As my heart seems ready to leap from my chest, I push off, sending the swing forward in a small arc. I'm not sure if I'm trying to calm my nerves or if I think that another monster might run past, but I stay there for the better part of ten minutes, and nothing happens.

No horrifying ogres stomp through the night, no pixies speed by, no illusory lights or spectral forms light up the sky. It's just a normal boring night in Toronto. If I didn't know any better, I'd think monsters weren't real, but I can't even pretend to have those doubts anymore. I saw one again. For the first time since I was a child.

The swing groans as I push off it, sprinting out of the playground, my hope renewed and certain that I'll find something. If not tonight, it'll happen. I'm going to see Roze again.

A light!

It's shining from across the street. I hurry to it. Could it be?

I come up short as a heavy wooden door closes, blocking off the light. Someone went inside. This couldn't be it, could it?

Above two stone pillars, a church proudly bears its name. Can they even set foot here? Maybe they don't invite vampires? Are they real? They'd have to be, right?

Unable to answer those questions, I take a deep breath, steady myself, and head right up to the door. At first, I consider knocking, but I won't take no for an answer. My heart beats in my throat as I grasp the metal handle of the door and give it a quick pull.

It comes right open. No dreadful force keeps me out, and no fangs sink into my throat when I take a tentative step inside. There aren't any monsters in the foyer, at least. "Hello?" I call, doubts creeping in. Am I breaking into this church? What if there really are monsters here, and they're not friendly? What am I going to do?

Another breath. In and out. In and out. I head on. There has to be someone here. I saw them. "Hello?" I call again, peering through doors and around corners.

Past the third door, in a long hallway with thick, sound-damp-ening carpets, I finally find an answer. An old man, at least a few decades past my father, if not my grandfather, stares at me, cocking his head. "Yes, can I help you?" His voice is soft, gentle, and human.

"Sorry," I offer, pointing behind me as if that offers any sort of explanation.

"Are you all right?"

My mouth opens and closes, and I look behind me, then back to him. A crease forms between his bushy gray eyebrows as he studies me.

"Ma'am?"

"Sorry. I just..." Another breath. "I got separated from my friends. I was trying to find them. I saw you and thought you may have seen them and..." I offer an awkward smile. I'm young, cute, and blond; it can get me out of a lot of problems. "I'm not sure what I was thinking. I'll leave you alone. Sorry."

He takes a few steps toward me, his green eyes radiating kindness. "Are you sure? Do you need something to drink? We have coffee, hot chocolate?"

I shake my head. "No. I'm sorry. I'll get out of your hair."

He hesitates for a moment before nodding. "Very well. Service is at seven. Any chance I'll see you there?"

"I'll think about it," I offer as genuinely as I can manage.

"Well, I hope you'll be there."

I give another smile and spin around, trying to keep to a walking pace as I hurry out. That could've been bad. I'm glad it was a church. What if I'd broken into, I don't know, a drug…place? Den? I wouldn't even know what to tell people then. I've never—well, there was that one time—but there were no criminals or anything. What if they had a gun?

Am I really more worried about drug dealers than actual monsters?

I hold my face in my hands, and tears start falling. I don't even know why I'm crying. Maybe I didn't get enough sleep. What is wrong with me?

I blink the tears away, shaking my head and staring out at the night. If you can even call it that. Pink colors the horizon to my left.

Chewing on my lip, I try to consider my options. Should I have asked him if he'd seen any monsters? No, I'd sound crazy. I can't ask around, can I? Maybe I should try.

But there's no one else to ask.

Right across the street, there's a hotel with a few lights shining inside. Maybe they'd have something?

I hurry over—there are no cars on the street to avoid—and head into the office. There's no one behind the counter, but before I have time to second guess myself, a middle-aged woman comes in from the back. "Hi, sorry, are you a guest here?"

"No. I…" I purse my lips. What am I going to say? Have you seen any monsters around? Have there been any strange black-market gatherings around here? The hell am I doing? I don't know the first thing about tracking down a secret monster society. Why don't they offer courses on this? "Have you seen anything strange?"

She blinks, brushing a long strand of red hair out of her eyes. "This is a bed and breakfast. I see a lot of strange things."

I'm not going to ask about that horned figure I saw. I'm not even sure I saw it. "What about, like, a lot of noise? From somewhere nearby but not in the hotel? Is there someplace where a lot of people gather late at night?"

Her eyes narrow as she rests her elbows on the counter, staring me down. "What are you talking about? Who did you say you were?"

Right. I need a better answer. There has to be something. I told the last guy that I'm looking for my friends. I can build on that. I take a deep breath, doing my best to look pained, like I can't quite bring myself to say it. "My friends...I...they've gotten into some trouble. At first, I thought it was only Caroline, but I've been noticing marks on both their arms."

The woman takes a deep breath.

"Right," I confirm. See, I know at least one thing about drugs. "They keep disappearing around here. I followed them tonight, hoping to confront them, but they got away. I don't know if they realized I was there or if I just missed a turn they made. I lost them a couple blocks from here, and I thought maybe..." My voice breaks, and I pinch my nose, blinking hard, trying to make my eyes water. "Maybe there's someplace around here where they were shooting up? I think that's the term, at least. I'm in over my head. Please, Miss, what was your name?"

"Evans."

"Ms. Evans, please, if there's anything that you know..." I take in a shaky breath. I'm not bad at this. I do my best not to smile from my own praise. "Is there someplace where people seem to gather at night around here, or where there've been a bunch of loud partiers or people breaking stuff? Anything you might know that could help."

She starts to shake her head but hesitates, squinting as she reconsiders. "Now that you mention it..." She sighs. "I'm not sure that it's anything, but there's been a lot of weird vandalism all over. My family has run this place for, God, that would be aging myself, for decades, and this only started, maybe ten, twelve years ago? Long enough that I've gotten used to it, but it drove prices down. There are weird marks sometimes. Like the walls get scratches on them, or occasionally, I'll see bite marks in toys that get left outside. Maybe it's a dog fighting ring, I don't know."

"Do you know where it is?"

Ms. Evans shakes her head. "I'm afraid not. I've seen groups sometimes, all in hoodies, but they've never actually done anything, and they're usually gone within a second of my noticing them. I'm sorry I couldn't tell you more. I really hope you find them."

It's enough. At least this should mean I'm looking in the right place. I hope. "Thank you." I give her a pained grin and start to head out.

"Would you like some coffee?"

I start to say no, but I am running off two hours of sleep, and this time, I didn't break in. "Sure. I'd really appreciate it."

"It's no problem. I only hope my daughters have a friend who cares as much you do."

This time, I don't have to force my smile. I'm lying about the whole thing, but it's still really sweet.

She hands me a steaming, foamy cup of coffee, and I dump half a dozen packets of sugar into it. Canadian coffee is awful, and if it doesn't taste like candy, then I don't see the point. I wish her a good day and head back outside, blowing on the cup so I can finally take a sip.

My phone rings in my pocket. I probably should've silenced that for sneaking around. I flip it open. "Hey, Caroline," I say, hoping my voice doesn't go through the door. That would make my lie much more apparent. I hurry along, whispering, "What's up?"

"I need to head back. My class starts in forty minutes."

"You can head on. I'll meet up with Taya."

"I don't want to go back on my own!"

I roll my eyes. "You've already been walking on your own."

"Yeah, but, please?"

I sigh. At least I know I'm in the right area. Probably. Maybe. "Fine. Let me call Taya, and we can all meet back up outside that pub."

"Thank you."

I call her while I walk and explain the situation. "But we're in the middle of a monster hunt," Taya whines.

"I know."

"Fine," she grumbles. "You can't just spring the existence of the supernatural on a girl and expect her to go back to class like everything is normal."

"Apparently, Caroline can."

Still grumbling, she grunts an affirmative. "Fine. I'll be there. But we're looking more later."

"We are," I confirm. It's like looking for a needle in a haystack, but at least I know the needle is there. I'll find it. I just need to keep looking, and at least I have help.

Unfortunately, that later isn't today. We both pass out in my bed the second we get back, and I end up having to hurry to class, late and un-showered, only to fall back asleep when my classes are over. I'll probably have better luck if I've slept anyway.

CHAPTER TWELVE

ROZE

It's been years. Who else can I possibly ask about this? What else can I do?

Futures change like the leaves, and yet this one is so immutable. I can't tell them the reason I need to change it—I can't tell anyone what it is—and even if I could, what difference would it make? I have tried every last thing I can think of to change it. I'm truly lost. What am I to do?

I collapse in a clearing, a brook babbling on as if it has any answers to give. I care so much about her, I need her in my life, but with what's to happen, there's no way I can do that.

I have to change things.

But I can't just not talk to her.

Tears fall from my eye, and the clear sky above turns to rain. I watch it form endless ripples in the water, blinking away the blurs as they come. If my grandmother didn't have an answer, then that's that.

I squeeze my eye shut, pressing my hand to it and pulling my knees to me. I curl myself into as small a ball as I can and continue to cry the rain.

No child calls for my help.

No newborn needs their future told.

There's nothing to distract me from my fears.

As the last drop of rain falls, I lie back in the soft damp grass, its scent filling the air, and I do my best to focus. I know the issue. I know it all too well. And yet, if I can't fix it, then that raises another all too important question. Why?

Why do I care so much? Why do I refuse to give up on my friendship with her when I know what it will cost? Am I just so selfish that I could...

Raindrops splash in the brook.

She's my oldest friend. That's all there is to it. That's all I'll let there be to it. Every year, I look forward to when I get her letter. I spend months perfecting exactly what I'll say to her, what she needs to know. Those days mean the world to me, and I could never go without them. Even if it means...what?

If it means risking everything? That I would betray my kind just for her? I won't. I can't. No matter how selfish I am, that's simply not me. I'm a laume, and I will not do that to my family. They need me. They need all of us.

I sigh, running fingers through the blond locks in front of my eye. I suppose I have my answer.

CHAPTER THIRTEEN

DOVANA

I open my eyes, blinking away the newly risen sun. How long was I asleep? Goddamn it. I lost almost an entire day that I should've spent searching. What am I going to do? I have to find a way to find her.

Shaking my head, I sit up, blinking rapidly as I try to rid myself of the lingering effects of sleep. I barely even remember my dream, but I know she was there.

I know I have all the time in the world, but it's been so long, and I need to see her in person again. Even if I don't quite understand why. She means so much to me, and now that I know I can actually spend time with her, I will stop at nothing to make it so.

On the off chance it'll work, I set out a few slices of bread— we're out of honey wheat, so hopefully, white will do—and hop in the shower. By the time I'm dry and dressed, nothing has touched the bread. I give it another hour while I check up on social media on my laptop. Since I'm already online, I may as well start my search here.

I try looking up monster sightings in Toronto, but that naturally gets me nothing useful, so I pull up a map and look around the area I was searching yesterday. If I was a monster, where would I hang out?

Not at the church or the bed and breakfast. Maybe that pub? No, I was told they congregate at night, and that's when it's open, so people would see something. Hell, I'd have seen something when I went there.

There're a few sorority houses, a day care, a park, a few apartments, and some sort of management place. I click on it. They only lease apartments. I could see demons being involved in it, I suppose, but it doesn't match what I was told. That's certainly not the kind of place you'd see partying, though maybe after hours?

I exit out of it and click on a few nearby buildings. Wait. The public school? They wouldn't, would they? It would be big enough, it closes early enough, and it even has a big kitchen. I don't know. I'm probably leaping to conclusions. And it's not like I can look into it before tonight, but I'm gonna check there first. I think it's my best bet.

The plate on the windowsill clatters, and I nearly jump out of my seat as I go to take a look. A startled bird flaps its wings, caws at me, and picks up the bread before flying off. Great. Not quite what I was looking for.

With a heavy groan, I hold my face in my hands, dropping back into bed. I'm going about this all wrong. I need more information, but how? If no fair one is willing to show up, then who can I ask? Am I just supposed to grab a Ouija board?

Well...

No. I shake my head. Even if they work, it doesn't mean they'd have or give useful information. I need to keep searching. "Caroline?" I ask, looking over at her sleeping form.

A sleepy groan answers me. "It's Saturday," she says a moment later, covering her head with her pillow.

I chew my lip. I've already slept like twelve hours. I need to be out there. "So you don't have anything better to do."

"Vana."

With a heavy sigh, I lean back, lacing my fingers behind my head. "I have to find her."

"I know you do. And I'll help, but it's not an emergency, and I have a life."

I start to snap at her but catch myself. She's right. This hasn't been eating at her for the last fifteen years, and she was already late for class because of me and got almost no sleep. "But you'll help more soon?"

The pillow falls to the floor, and she meets my eyes, her brown eyes surprisingly warm as she nods. "Yes. You know I will. I've always got you, Vana. I'll even go with you tonight if you want, but until then, let me sleep a bit longer. I need to have the energy for shopping this afternoon."

"Shopping?" I haven't gone in a while, but I don't have it in me to be that excited. I want to find Roze. Granted, looking cute would be a nice bonus, but it's not what I'm looking for right now. It's not like I'm trying to win her heart. I just want to see my friend.

"That salon at the Honeydale Mall is having a sale. I can't think of the name right now. Rachel and I are going. You're welcome to come."

I mull that over. It's far from where the monsters are supposed to be, and I should be out there. But on the other hand, I can't exactly find them in the middle of the day. "But we can get back to looking right after dinner?"

Her giggle always sounds comforting. "Yes. But now that I know you're rich, you're buying us dinner."

"I'm not rich."

"How much gold do you have just in this room?"

"I'll pay for dinner."

I tap my chopsticks on my plate. There's one piece of sashimi left and some rice, but the mix of excitement and anxiety in my belly leaves little room for food. I pull my laptop out of my backpack. I want to work on that essay for my Ancient Philosophy course, but once I find out they have wireless, I go right back to my map. That school really does seem the best chance. It's one of the biggest buildings around, if I don't count the apartments as a single building. They're not built as one, and people live in them, so the monsters couldn't all party together.

"We're going to look soon," Taya says, using her sleeve to wipe soy sauce from her cheek. "Take your time and eat."

"But—"

She silences me with a glare. I swear, ever since we were a couple, she always thinks she has to look after me. I can look after myself. "We'll find your fairy."

"Fair one."

"We'll find your fucking laume, you..." She groans, gritting her teeth. "Eat. Grab a few more plates, maybe even have some ice cream or something. If we're going to be running around town for the rest of the night, you need more than, like, four pieces of sushi in you."

"Five."

That same glare. Great. Fine. I snatch another plate from the conveyor belt, and when that seems to do nothing for her glare, I grab another. "Look for who?" Rachel asks.

I offer an awkward grin to the little redhead as I try to come up with an explanation. I've only met her a couple times before, so I'm not exactly keen on sharing all the magical details of my life yet.

"An old friend of hers," Caroline says. "We just found out that she moved to town, but we don't have her address or phone number."

"Oh, have you tried the school registry?"

"She's not a student," I reply.

"Google?"

If only. "She doesn't even have a Facebook account."

"The fuck?" Her jaw drops, and the California roll falls back onto her plate. "How? What?"

She's also not actually in town, but I appreciate Caroline's lie too much to point that out. "She's old-fashioned."

"Is she a Mennonite or something?"

Caroline and Taya both chuckle, but I'm too flabbergasted to join them. If only Taya had had the sense not to bring Roze up right here. "No, she's from the old country and didn't grow up as well-off as my family did." I'm sure plenty of people don't even know that Lithuania has electricity; she'll buy any lie I tell about it.

"Oh." She seems to accept that. I thought I'd at least have to say more. "Oh, Caroline, did you do the take-home test for Prof. Werner's class? Because I have no idea what I'm doing."

"Did you look over the book?"

She grins. "Nope."

Caroline rolls her eyes and pushes up her glasses. "We're busy tonight, but I can help you with it tomorrow if you really need."

"Oh, you're going with her? Can I come?"

We all look at each other, searching for words. I try to come up with a believable excuse.

"No," Caroline says flatly. "You have to actually try the test first if you want my help."

"But—"

"Tomorrow. I promise."

"Fine," she grumbles, giving her California roll another attempt. "Oh, thanks for the sushi, Dove…Vana," she attempts.

I shrug. "It's no problem."

We finish up our meals, ready for the big hunt, and I take care of the bill, leaving a nice tip. Now we can finally get back to my search. And I can see Roze again.

Chapter Fourteen

Roze

My steps don't take me to my mother. I was looking for her. I'm not sure what I was going to tell her; perhaps I was going to finally come clean, or maybe I simply wanted to be with someone who loves me now that I have my answer. That's how it works, though. I know where I need to be, and I walk, and the woods take me there. I already decided. Don't tell me that my doubts are trying to drag me elsewhere.

This isn't even what I do. I rescue children, and I tell the future. Sewing and housework have never been part of my calling. Why would I find myself at this cabin? Who even still lives in a cabin in the woods? I know my grandmother grew up with that, but these days, people tend to live in the cities or at least small towns.

Ignoring the cottage, I turn and continue walking. I'll talk to my mother. Maybe I'll even sort out what I want to tell her. She deserves to know about Dovana, and I need to tell her that I won't let it control me. Even if it means I have to…I sigh, barely able to bring the words to mind.

Then I blink. I'm no closer to my mother. I'm at the entrance to the cabin. I was very specifically walking away from this.

With another sigh, I grit my teeth and walk up to the door. No sound or smell comes from inside. It seems utterly empty. There's not even the telltale scent of a *zaltys* or an aitvaras. I've never seen a house so empty or unprotected in my home country.

They really do need someone to look after them.

I give the door a tug and find that there's nothing locking it; it comes right open. A small mess greets me. Dust on the floor, dirty plates on the table and in the sink, and a basket of clothes near overflowing. Nothing unreasonable, they hardly need a laume to come and rescue them from it, but clearly, something needs me here. Even if it's only me that needs it.

I get to work. Scrubbing the plates takes only a few minutes, and soon they're dried and sparkling from their place in the cabinets. I've more of a knack for this work than I thought, as I seem to know precisely where everything goes. It's only when I start searching for a way to wash the clothes that I realize they don't have a washing machine. I find a washbasin outside, along with a washboard, and start going through the clothes.

It would be tiring work for a mortal, but we laumes were made for this. Unfortunately, the work is repetitive and mindless and leaves me with far too much time to think.

She's my best friend. It's been fifteen exhausting years of trying to change this, of looking for any out, and there's nothing I can do. If I don't want to betray my kind, then I have to forget her, but I don't know if I can.

No. Ruta and Smilte already gave me all the reminders I need. My duty shall always be to my family. Not to a human girl. It can't be to her. Ever.

The fabric strains as I scrape it across the board, and by the time I realize what's happening, there's a tear up the side of one dress. I set it aside and finish the rest before finding a needle and thread and fixing it, then hanging it up to dry with its companions.

I pantomime wiping sweat from my brow. I don't sweat, but there is a splash of soapy water there, so the action was less of an affectation than I'd thought. I find a mop in the back of a closet, and start bringing the floor to a matte shine. It's all hardwood and looks both new and well taken care of, so the work is easy. To prevent myself from thinking of anything too important, I consider what I was reading in Kierkegaard's writing. I'd found another copy in a store in Vilnius, and having it in a language I'm more fluent in makes it much easier. Well, moderately easier. It's still a dense tome full of thoughts that I'd never considered. And it still speaks to me, much as it seems to speak to Dovana.

Surprisingly, focusing on the ideas of guilt and sin does little to ease my mind when considering losing my dearest and oldest friend or risking failing in my duty to my family. I knew I should've just read some Socrates.

Why am I even thinking about this if I'm considering not talking to her?

I slump against the wall as the weight of the world seems to rest upon my shoulders. This is all unfair. If only I couldn't see the future so well, then I wouldn't even have this decision to make.

Something creaks behind me. At first, I think nothing of it. It's a cabin in the woods, of course it's going to creak sometimes. Then I hear footsteps and voices. It occurs to me that I must seem an intruder.

I glance around, leaning the mop against the wall. Hiding isn't likely to make this look any less suspicious, but any look has to be better than having a pre-existential crisis in their hallway.

But as I glance about, I see something strange. There's a reason that they live out in the middle of nowhere. I hadn't thought to look at any of the photos on the wall or thought to wonder.

Admiring my work, or perhaps puzzling over it as he marvels at his reflection in the floor, is a tall, brown-haired, human man. And next to him, still holding his hand, his head several inches below the human's, stands a *kaukas*. The little household luck spirit, only he wasn't staying in the house. And they don't tend to interact with their humans like this.

"How did you even pull this off?" the human asks, stooping and kissing the little spirit. Well, that answers that.

To save what little awkwardness I can, I clear my throat. "My apologies. That was me, I meant to be gone by the time you were home."

"A laume?" the *kaukas* asks.

The man nods, rising, a grin slowly spreading across his face, only to turn into a bright chuckle. "That explains it. Well, thank you.

Lord knows neither of us was going to get to it anytime soon." He shoots his partner a jovial scowl.

"Speak for yourself. I'm the one who does most of the housework around here anyway. You simply lie about."

"I do not." He bumps his knee against the kaukas's shoulder.

I should leave. I should let them be. But how can this be? I don't know kaukas' culture very well, but they're house spirits; this has to go against everything they're taught. Well, it's not like I can leave without a word. "Sorry to barge in like this. I'm Roze, by the way."

The human gives me a warm smile. "It's no problem at all. You've saved us a lot of work. I'm Gedymin, and this is my husband, Paulius," he says, gesturing at the kaukas. "It's a pleasure to meet you."

My jaw drops, but I do my best to compose myself before I look too rude. I was never taught much in the way of manners, but it would hardly do to offend the ones I'm assisting. "It's wonderful to meet you as well," I stammer, doing my best to sound casual.

Paulius chuckles. "That must seem awfully queer to you."

"No." I wave my hands in front of me as if trying to shove away the completely accurate accusation. "It's nothing like that. Of course not. I just…I mean I was surprised but certainly nothing like finding it outlandish." Because that absolutely makes me sound better. I glance between the wry grins the two men are giving me. My goose is thoroughly cooked, so I may as well take it out. I think that's how the expression goes. I don't have an oven or eat meat, so it never really seemed to apply. "And your families allow this?"

Gedymin laughs, but it seems far less jovial than his prior expression. "It's a little complicated."

"It isn't." Paulius shoots back, staring up. "It's almost too simple, really." He pulls out a chair and plops down. "There a reason you ask?"

My eyes widen, and I fiercely shake my head, offering a vehement, "No," before adding a calmer, "I'm just curious."

"Mm-hmm," he muses, stroking the graying beard that almost reaches his belly. "Well, you've seen where we live. We're well away from either of our families and with good reason."

The human man leans against his kitchen counter—now polished to a shine—shaking his head. "We don't need to go over this again."

"It sounds like she might need to know."

"No! I don't. Never mind me. Forget it."

A throatier and more genuine laugh comes from the kaukas, his round belly shaking with it. "I'm sure you know how it is. We're an all but forgotten people, and we can't allow our kind to die out. We must go find a mate and produce children. I assume your parents told you something similar?"

I nod, staring, scarcely able to breathe a word.

"There are other options. And I told them so, but they didn't care. I'd have been willing to at least make a kid real quick if they needed, nice and proper, but they didn't even want that by the time I finally left. They felt I was bringing shame to our entire race. It was not proper. It was not done. Running off with a human was already forbidden, but a man?" He shakes his head. "But I knew I'd never be happy if I stayed with them and ignored who I was and who I loved. I don't know what it's like living with laumes. Maybe they wouldn't be as cruel. Womenfolk do tend to be much more caring, after all."

"There's nothing to tell them," I shout. Why does he keep dragging me into this?

"I only meant in general."

Gritting my teeth, I suck in a breath. Fine, there's something to tell them, but it's not that. Even if I was in love with Dovana, and I'm not, I wouldn't be running off with her. I'm not like him. I'm nothing like him. "Well, I would never abandon my family either way."

Gedymin holds out his hands, stepping between the two of us. "Woah. She's a guest, Paulius, how about we don't put her on the spot."

"You think I abandoned them?" The ice in his voice would freeze even Blizgulis's offspring. "They abandoned me. They had a wealth of chances to keep me amongst them and threw them all away because I didn't conform to exactly what they wanted." He leaps down from the chair, taking a few steps toward me, stopping just short of Gedymin. "I did nothing wrong."

"Paulius…"

I meet him, towering over him. "You knew they needed you. They're your family. Your race. They should be your whole world. If we're not meeting our expectations, our duties, then what are we?"

The human finally turns on me. "Roze, we appreciate what you did, but please leave."

I bite down the bile rising in my throat as I meet that traitor's gaze. "I'm nothing like you. I won't do that to my people." I stomp out of the house, not bothering to listen to the kaukas's muttered curses. I don't know why I was brought here, but it has only hardened my resolve. My duty is to my family, and that's all. It has to be.

Chapter Fifteen

Dovana

We abandon Rachel at her dorm and drop off the bags of clothes in Caroline's and my room. It's a bit cold out, and I'm looking for any excuse to wear these new jeans, so I change into them, along with the purple button-up I found for seventy percent off, and then we finally head out.

"Thanks again," I say, as we head to the same area as the other night. We don't need to orient ourselves this time. We know exactly where we're going.

"Hey, I have to reunite you with your sugar momma," Taya says.

I roll my eyes. We've been over this enough already. "She's not my sugar mommy. She's my friend."

"Who gives you lots of money."

"I wish I had friends like that," Caroline adds.

I stuff my hands in my pockets, taking in a deep breath. "It really isn't like that. I haven't even seen her since we were kids. She isn't...I'm not...oh, just shut up."

Taya chuckles and pats me on the back. "I know. We'll find a way for you to contact her. Don't worry. I just hope we're not barking up the wrong tree."

I glance at her. "You mean the school?"

"I mean, I hope these monsters will have a way to contact her. It's not like the fairy did."

"Fae," I mutter.

Caroline glances back at me, idly toying with her brown ponytail. "Did you have anything planned for once you found them?"

"I just need information. Maybe they'll have some ritual or something, but at least they should know something about how I can get word to her."

"And you're sure you can't just wait until next year?" Taya asks. "You could tell her you want to meet up in your letter. Or snatch her from the window like you did the other night."

I groan. "If I have to, I will, but I've waited so long already, and I just want to see her again."

"I know. And you will. I just don't want you to get your hopes up. Even if we find the monster hangout place, it doesn't mean we'll find what we're looking for."

Nodding, I say, "You're right, but it's the only lead I have right now. You know, this is why people don't like Russian authors. You don't always have to be so pessimistic."

"I thought you described it more as nihilistic when you were reading Dostoevsky."

"It's depressing, whatever it is. Like, no other existential author bothers me near as much. *The Brothers Karamazov* is extremely good, but it's so melancholy. I've literally read about how freeing the idea of suicide is, and it's nothing like trying to get through his stuff."

"You just hate Russians."

Caroline stares at me. "What? How is suicide…what?"

I shrug. "Don't worry about it. Or just read some Camus. I really doubt you'd get into it."

"I wasn't planning on it."

"I mean Camus, not suicide."

She rolls her eyes. "Yes, I gathered."

"Just making sure."

We're almost to that bar we'd passed before. It had seemed much farther the other night. "Do we want to go in and check, grab a drink, ask people if they've seen monsters?"

"I'd rather not give people reason to think I'm crazy," Taya says. "Now, if we're going in for a drink, yes, I'll happily go in for at least six, but I don't think there are any monsters there."

I peer through the window. It's dark, but I can see people drinking, eating, and playing pool. No one has horns, wings, tails, or any other interesting appendages. They all look painfully human. "You don't think it's worth trying?"

"Be my guest. If you want to ask if they've seen any monsters running around town, you're more than welcome to."

"I've asked before about seeing anything weird or if there was anyone causing trouble."

"You actually talked to people?" Her expression shifts, but I'm not sure if she looks worried or impressed. "I just walked around dark alleys looking for anything weird or with a bunch of eyes. Probably not the best plan, now that I think about it. Maybe we shouldn't split up this time."

"I talked to someone," Caroline says. "But they just tried to sell me weed."

I glance again at the bar. If we go in, Taya will end up ordering drinks, and we'll all find nice warm spots at a booth and settle in, and we won't be searching. Or maybe I'm simply looking for an excuse not to do it. "Fine, we'll try on the way back."

"And then we can get drinks. It's the weekend. I don't have anything I need to do in the morning."

"Do you think the monsters are even out yet?" Caroline asks. "It's not even eight. It seems like more of a midnight thing."

I wish I knew anything here. How do I have so much experience with all this and still know so little? "Well, that fair one didn't say anything to suggest that."

"What time was it when you first saw Roze?" Taya asks.

Huh. I'm actually not sure. "Let me check." I flip open my phone and hold two to speed dial my mama.

She answers on the second ring. "Hey there, honey, I wasn't expecting to hear from you tonight. Is everything all right?"

"Yeah, I'm fine. I was wondering, what time of day was it when I got lost and met Roze?"

"What a weird question."

Should I tell her that I told Taya and Caroline? Of course I should. I've never lied to my mama—okay, well, I haven't lied to her since I had to explain why I smelled like pot that one time in high school—I'm not going to start now. "I told Caroline and Taya, and they both understand, and we're looking for a way to find her, and I wanted to know around when she was out doing stuff."

There's silence on the line for several long moments. "Okay, wow. That's a lot to take in. I thought Taya didn't believe you? She finally came around?"

"Yeah. I guess she's mellowed in her old age." Taya glares at me, and I stick out my tongue.

"Well, all right. Do you want me to help? I could drive you."

"It's okay. I just need the time."

She ignores me. "How're you looking for her? Please tell me you're in the library and not wandering the streets of downtown Toronto."

"Well…" I glance around. This probably counts as downtown. "I can also try the library?"

"I'll get my coat."

"No, Mama. It's okay. It's the three of us. We're fine."

"I'd still rather—"

"If we don't find anything tonight, then I'll call you first thing in the morning, and we can look together. But right now, I want to do this with my friends. Okay? I love you."

I can almost hear her staring at her car keys. She wants to ignore me and come help. But it'd be weird. I can't have my mother take over my quest. I'm looking for monsters. You don't bring your parents into that. "Fine. It was in the evening when you saw her. I was making dinner, so a little earlier than now. Are you sure? I could pick up food on the way."

"We already ate."

"And you'll call me tomorrow?"

"I promise."

"All right. Take care. If anything happens to you, I will never forgive you."

"I know."

"I love you, my dear gift." Wow, she really is worried. Or angry. It has to be one or the other. She never calls me that unless she needs to remind herself. "Tomorrow?"

"Yes, Mama."

"Okay. Have fun scouring the dangerous streets for signs of the fae."

Wow, it sounds crazy when she says it like that. "Have fun looking after Matis."

"I will. He actually wants me around."

Now that's just not true. "Good-bye, Mama."

"Just take care of yourself."

"I will. Bye," I repeat.

"Good-bye." She sounds so pained.

I close the phone and stuff it back in my pocket. "She says it was even earlier than now. So if they work like her, we should be able to find whatever monsters there are."

"All right, then. Let's go search that school," Caroline says, leading the charge.

❖

I give the doorknob a hesitant pull. If this is where all the monsters hang out, then it would be unlocked, right? That makes sense. It doesn't move, and neither do any of the other three doors at this entrance. "The hell?" Caroline asks. "They always left the doors open."

"What do you mean?" Taya asks.

"In high school, we used to break in here at night. Me and a few friends who went here when they were kids. This entrance was always unlocked, and the stairs were all covered in graffiti. You could easily come in and do whatever you wanted. Not that I did. I mean, nothing bad."

"Of course, you were an upstanding kid."

"I was an honor student. I am an honor student."

I chuckle. "Then what did you come in here for?"

Her cheeks color, and she does her best to hide them by turning her back to us and hunching her shoulders, staring hard at the door as if she can will it open. "Nothing."

"Ah," Taya says knowingly.

"It wasn't like that."

"Of course not. You just broke in here to study."

"Yes! Exactly." She smiles hopefully at us.

Taya claps her on the shoulder. "Who were you studying with?"

"No one!"

"Well, now, that is weird," I say, joining in. I should really go easy on her. I know how difficult it can be to argue with Taya, but Caroline keeps blushing so bright, and I can't help it. "I had no idea you were such an exhibitionist. Just needed that air of risk when you were studying all by yourself?"

"No." She spins back around, trying all of the doors again. "Let's try the other side."

"This is more fun," Taya says.

I roll my eyes. "Come on, we've tormented her enough. We need to find a way in."

"There's a hole in the fence over here. No one ever went in that way, but maybe…" Caroline stops short, staring at the fence surrounding the back of the school. "It was right here."

"It's been a few years," Taya says. "Things change."

"Unless, you think it's the monsters?" I ask. "They could've amped up security so that people couldn't walk right in. Especially after a few too many kids came in to study."

"Hey!"

Taya has to clutch her belly she's laughing so hard. "No wonder you were an honor student, all that time studying."

"I will go home."

She holds up her hands. "Fine. Fine. Help me up?"

Caroline stares at her.

"Put your hands out and boost me over. I'll look around."

"How will you get back?" I ask.

"Do you think you can even climb the fence?"

Taya sighs. "Dovana can vouch for me. I'm very flexible."

Great, now I'm the one blushing.

"Oh, did you take ballet back in Russia?" She holds her hands out, still studying the hole-less fence.

I suck in a breath through my teeth.

Taya stomps forward as she glares. "You think all Russians learn ballet? Like, that's just something over there?"

"What? No?"

"And you think we all get drugged up to make it to the Olympics too, don't you?"

"Oh, don't try to deny that one," I call. "If you lot could just stop cheating, people wouldn't call you out on it so much."

She puts her foot on Caroline's outstretched hands, pushing down hard enough that the poor thing winces. "That's just how Russians are. No steroids needed."

"Right," I say, absolutely genuinely and sincerely.

Caroline pushes up on her feet. "Would you jump already?"

Taya pulls her free foot back, then pushes off the ground. As Caroline raises her hands, Taya leaps off, grasping the top of the fence and managing to swing her leg over. Chuckling, she sits on the top, looking down at us. "I started taking gymnastics once I moved out here." She slides down a few inches, then drops, bending her knees and rolling on impact.

Caroline offers polite applause.

Taya runs around the side of the building, and the two of us are left waiting on our own.

"What if she finds a monster?" Caroline asks.

"She'll be fine," I say, trying to sound more convinced than I feel. I've been trying hard to avoid that lingering fear, but we're all putting our lives at risk. And for what? For the chance that I might see my friend again? Yeah, apparently. "Are you sure you want to keep doing this?"

"It's only the second day."

"Yeah, but…" I sigh. "I don't want either of you to be hurt."

A sudden tug on my hand pulls me off balance, and for an instant, I think I'm done for when I finally see Caroline holding my hand. "I want to help. After everything I've already seen and everything you've told me, I would feel awful if I didn't. Roze means a lot to you, and if I can help you two reconnect, then I have to. You're my friend too, Dovana, even if I've only known you for a few months."

I nod. "Thank you. That really means a lot. You're my friend too, Caroline. And I'm very glad I have you."

She beams back at me.

The fence rattles behind us, and we nearly jump out of our skins. "Hey," Taya says, grinning like a rabid dog as we both clutch our chests. "Sorry, I didn't mean to scare you."

"You sure seem to be enjoying it," Caroline snaps back.

Taya chuckles. "The gate was locked, as were all the doors. But I looked in the windows, and there didn't seem to be any movement inside. I think they may have just improved the school's security since your studying days."

While Caroline blushes and stammers, I say, "Let's just drop it. So there's nothing here?"

She shakes her head. "It sure doesn't seem it. I can't say for sure, since I didn't manage to get in, but I don't think it's the place."

"Do you want to turn back?" I ask, looking between them.

"The night's still young," Taya says.

Caroline cleans her glasses on her blouse, glares at them, and cleans them again. "No, I'm fine. Let's keep going."

Feeling a bit dejected, we stroll up a dark alley, heading toward the park. No monster jumps out and grabs us, unfortunately. I really thought we looked delicious too. "Where are we going to look now? The school seemed like it had to be the place. It was a sure bet."

"What about this church?" Taya says, pointing. "That would be really ironic. I'm sure some monsters must have a sense of humor."

"Roze has a nice one."

"Would she do it?"

I shrug, chewing my lip. "Maybe, but I already looked in there yesterday."

"Oh, right, you said," Caroline says. "And I checked the park up there. It would be nearly impossible to hide something like this out in the open like that anyway. It has to be indoors."

"Yeah. He said a round building. But I'm not sure how much that tells us. Do we knock on every door in the apartment complexes?" Taya asks. "It's kind of roundish. Maybe."

I glance at the nearby one. I think there's another a block or two over, but this one alone looks like it'd take a while. I suppose between the three of us, it wouldn't be that long. I check my phone. "It's only nine o'clock. I guess it's not that unreasonable."

"Let's say we're raising money for the school's hockey team. That sounds pretty believable."

"Shouldn't we have some forms, maybe a clipboard, anything to look like we're not trying to rip people off?" Taya asks.

Caroline nods. "We could go to the student center. It's like twenty minutes from here. We could print off a quick form, probably grab some clipboards, and hurry back to canvas the neighborhood."

"It'd be ten o'clock by the time we're back, though." I grind my heel into the pavement, trying to sort out the best course of action.

"We'll do that tomorrow," Taya says. "I like this new devious side of you, by the way, Caroline."

She tosses her ponytail back, smirking proudly. "You never let yourself find out how cool I could be."

"I'm glad you two are finally bonding, but if we're not doing the apartments, then where are we checking tonight?"

"Right, that." Taya groans. "Do we want to call it a night? We can start fresh first thing tomorrow after sundown."

Caroline shakes her head. "No. It's still early. We have time. We should at least look a little more."

"Oh, have you fallen in love with our Vana's girlfriend too?"

"She's not my—"

"And I don't swing that way," Caroline says. "Sorry to disappoint you."

She chuckles. "Well, my loss, I'm sure. Should we split up?"

"I'd really rather not. Hunting for monsters all night on my own is a lot less fun."

"She's right," I say. "There's safety in numbers. At least for now, we can stick together."

"Well, then, where to?"

"Why don't we just walk?" I ask. "It's not like we have any better ideas, and standing around isn't likely to help too much."

Taya stuffs her hands in her pockets and starts heading down the sidewalk. "Sure, why not? Come on."

Caroline and I fall into step behind her, glancing around at the Toronto nightlife, which isn't much for this part of town. There are a few drunk college kids and two people arguing over a hockey match on TV outside of a bar, and that's about it. We pass that bed and breakfast where I gave the story about Caroline's drug habit. Now we're looking somewhere new, ignoring that we're still across from one of the parks that Caroline was at. We would be the worst search and rescue team.

Taya sets her hand on her hip, looking around. Something smelled a little odd, but it may just be the stench of urine coming from the nearby alley.

"Can we not stop here?" Caroline asks.

But I spot something. Up there, could it really be that simple? "What did that pixie call them again? He didn't say monsters, right? I'm not going crazy."

"Demons?" Taya suggests.

"No, it wasn't demons," Caroline says. "He called them fiends."

I nod. "He said 'where all the fiends in town like to congregate.'"

"Right." She grins at me.

I point up at the sign in front of a little Quaker building that I would've never considered. The building is pretty round.

"House for Friends?" Taya asks.

"The 'r' is missing," Caroline points out.

"They wouldn't really, right?"

Taya shakes her head. "No. Of course not. That wouldn't make any sense. People would realize."

"Would they?" Caroline asks. "'Cause, I swear I've walked past this building dozens of times and never even noticed that the letter was gone."

"Yeah, but..." She stares up at it. "You don't think?"

"We might as well go and check." I take a deep breath, steel myself for the worst, and charge forward.

The building is set in from the road, with some tall shrubberies blocking it off from easy viewing. This might be the perfect place for a black market. We reach the front door without being murdered, so I take in another breath, let it out, in again, stop procrastinating, and turn the doorknob.

It opens right up and lets us in.

Chapter Sixteen

Roze

Still fuming, I go back to walking. I'll talk to my mother, I'll tell her everything about Dovana, and that I intend to keep my commitment to my family, and that will be that.

But the path keeps fighting me. It's as if there's someplace else I need to be, and no matter how hard I try, it keeps carrying me there. I step one foot in some woods in Vilnius and the next foot in Toronto, the next step in Babtai, and then I'm back in Canada. I can't get her out of my head.

Well, too bad, it doesn't matter. I don't care how set my fate is. It can't happen if I fulfill my purpose. I am a good laume and will serve and continue my family lineage. That is my fate, not whatever I keep seeing when I consider hers. I won't even let myself think of it.

And I'm back in Toronto.

I let out a wordless scream. I'm standing in this pitiful little park in the middle of the city. There's a bed and breakfast across the way and nothing of interest anywhere. What the hell is happening to me?

My next step is in Kedainiai, and I use every ounce of willpower to make the next one there as well. And the next. And the next. I will stay exactly where I intend to be. My powers and my life are mine to control, not the other way around.

With every movement, I will myself to where I wish to be. I will stay home, I will see my mother, I will discuss this all with her, and I will not run off to Toronto. I go once a year, and that's it, and it hasn't even been a week. No matter how much I miss her, it doesn't change a thing. I have a duty I must fulfill, and I shall do precisely that.

Finally, though it's like wading through a blizzard, I feel myself growing near. My mother must be at work. Rather than her favorite tree in the woods, I find myself outside of a small house in the southern end of Uzupe. The building looks even more run-down than the cottage I was at earlier, but it has a certain coziness to it. Curtains with different patterns line each window, while an ornate garden sits out front, and gray tiles line the roof, cracks showing in them.

I try peering in, but the decorative curtains block out more than I'd expected, and all I can make out inside is motion. So I walk right in. This is my purpose, and no house can keep me out.

As I suspected, I see my mother dumping trash into the refuse bin and singing an old song about the storm. If she keeps up that dancing, one might just come.

I fall into step beside her, assisting with cleaning as I try to sort out my thoughts.

"Roze," she calls excitedly. "I thought I felt you here. I can't believe you're finally giving our other arts a chance."

I shrug, focusing on scrubbing a spot out of a dish.

She bounds over to me as I finish and starts drying. "What brings you here? I know you've never felt the call to it before."

"I felt it earlier today for the first time," I say, ignoring the question. I've already made up my mind, so why is it still hard to come clean?

"Did you? And did you enjoy it? Our arts are all that culture has deemed to give women. It's wonderful to see you finally embracing all the variety there is to it."

I shrug again. "I didn't find it to my taste. My calling came to me naturally, and it's truly all I've ever wanted. This life is all I've ever wanted."

"I know, dear. I don't mean to push you to change."

My reflection stares back at me in the newly cleaned sink. "I met the people at the house I was called to. Well, I say people, one of them wasn't."

"Oh?"

What am I doing? "It was surprising to see. I thought there were so few of us left. As low as our numbers have been the last century, I can't help but marvel when I meet a fair one who I haven't already known."

She nods, grinning. "Of course. Every time I've convinced myself that I know every last one of us, I find one more who's managed to survive all this time. We're endangered, but we're still far from extinct, my dear child. You needn't worry your precious head so."

"Mustn't I? If we don't make sure to keep our population going, then that'll be it. If I don't fear for the future of our kind, we won't just be endangered, Mother. There are few laumes left and just as few fae who we can still reproduce with. One of them running off with a human…what am I to think, Mother?"

Her arms wrap around me, her fingers trailing through my hair as she holds my head to her shoulder. "Perhaps I've always trusted the future too much to you. Just because you can see it doesn't mean that you can change it. We'll fight for survival, of course we will, but what matters most is making use of the time we have. You can't resent those who reject the needs of their species for the needs of their heart."

I pull away, staring, my mouth opening and closing as I search for anything to say. "How could I ever think such a thing? We are family, all of us, and turning your back on family is simply unimaginable. It's wrong. For every one we lose, it's a future that we cannot make."

"The future is already made, my child."

"I've changed it before. so many times."

"Small things, yes, but not the course of an entire species. Not even your grandmother can do that."

"Well, we still don't know what will happen. No one can see the future of the fae. Even when Grandmother attempted a spell, it told her nothing we didn't know. Perhaps we can still save us. There may be enough, or perhaps Vaiva herself will return on her rainbow with a whole new litter of children. We don't have to die out. We don't have to lose everything."

She squeezes me back into the hug. "We still have many years, perhaps even centuries, before we'll have to find out. You needn't carry the weight of the world on your shoulders, my dearest child. Don't allow your family to become a burden. We're meant to be your strength, my flower."

Gritting my teeth, I pull away, staring at the sparkling floor. "You don't understand. You don't know the future I've seen. How I'm meant to betray you, the secret I've had to keep, I…something's wrong." The sensation is so overwhelming, it nearly sends me to my knees. I have to save someone. But it feels different, not only more intense, but it's wrong somehow. There's no child lost in the forest, awaiting my help. But nonetheless, someone I must rescue is in danger. "Do you feel that?" I ask.

"Feel what? Are you unwell?"

I shake my head, prying free from her renewed grasp. "I have to go. She's in danger." That's it. That's what's strange. That's why my path kept leading me astray. I have to rescue Dovana.

"Roze?"

"I'll see you soon, Mother. I can't waste time." I rush off, already back in that park across from the bed and breakfast. I won't let anything happen to her. I can't.

The feeling is so powerful, I could pinpoint her halfway across the world. I suppose I just did. I make a beeline for a small inset building across the road. I try walking in, my usual way, but it doesn't work. I've no power here. This isn't what I'm meant to do. But I'll still save her.

I have to circle around, running as fast as I can to find the door, but it opens right up, and I dash in. I blink, my jaw dropping as I take in the strange sight before me.

I'd expected humans. I can't imagine why they would be a threat to Dovana, but I was sure it would be something mundane, perhaps a mugger. Not…whatever this is.

The building is small, deceptively so, as it does not seem capable of holding so many. I can't tell if there are more rooms, but in just this one, there's hardly space to breathe. People, no, monsters are gathered around, shopping, talking, and...I gulp. Is that a slave auction? Are they bidding on humans? But we're meant to protect them. How could they? Why would they?

My vision blurs, and I do my best to blink away tears. From everything Dovana has told me, this drawback is far less severe when you're bi-ocular.

She's not in the auction. I don't know what to do about that, but I'm here to save one person in urgent danger. We can sort out the rest when she's safe.

I sense her across the room, though I still don't know how. Horns, tails, wings, and more limbs in more varieties than I can name block my way. The throng seems countless. How do they handle this? Or am I simply too used to the country, where I'm unlikely to encounter more than a handful of people on my path.

Shoving my way through, I hurry toward her and run headlong into something solid and heavy. An ogre glances down at me. "Pardon me," he says. "Are you all right?"

"Uh, yes. I'm fine."

"I'm sorry. I wasn't watching where I was going."

"It's okay," I say, doing my best to maintain my composure. Causing trouble won't help me.

He smiles. "Are you new here?"

"I am. But I'm meeting someone. I have to hurry. I'm sorry." With that, I go around him, having to duck to avoid someone's tail only to have a wing thwack me in the face. How do they put up with this?

I force my way past, and I can feel Dovana closer. "We weren't trying to cause any trouble." Is that her voice? It's been so long since I heard it.

"We're here to do some shopping, same as everyone else," another voice says.

"Well, I think you look a bit more likely to go on the menu."

"You don't really...you're joking, right?" An awkward chuckle follows that remark.

I can finally see them only for a griffin to step on my foot. Clutching it in pain, I hop forward and see claws dig into the shoulder of the dark-haired woman to Dovana's left. The little brunette squeaks in fear. "Please. We're not looking for trouble," Dovana insists.

"Unhand her," I call. Because that's going to help.

The hungry monster looks to me, confusion clear on his face. "She's free game." He cocks his head, looking me up and down. "No one's claimed her, and you know the rules for humans here. They go on the menu or in the auction."

"I've claimed her," I state with as much conviction as I can muster.

"What do you mean you—"

"You don't smell her?" What a creepy question, but I have to keep this up if I don't want her to die. "My coins are in their possession. I've given these girls my favor, and I'll not have you harm those in my care, you...you"—I don't know what he is—"monster."

"The hell did you call me?" Fangs bare as he wheels on me, a companion holding him back.

"You know the rules," the more sensible one says.

"But she called me a monster. There has to be an exception."

I just glare at them. I'm not going to risk saying something even worse.

"She probably doesn't know the rules. Listen to her accent."

"But—"

"Just come off it, Julian."

He growls, snapping at the air. "Don't think I'll forget this, fairy."

As much as I take offense at that remark, I've no time for it. "What the hell is going on?" I whisper.

The two women I don't recognize stare at me.

Dovana, on the other hand, runs to me, throwing her arms around me. "You're here. You're really here. I knew if I could just get here, then I'd find you. I didn't know how I'd do it, but I knew it would happen. It's been so long, Roze." I feel her shudder as a tear falls on my arm.

I find myself crying as well. "I've missed you too," I say, holding her tight. Vaiva, why have I put this off? "I'm so sorry I took so long."

"You made it in time. We're okay."

"I mean, all this time. I'm sorry. I should've seen you sooner."

Her hug only tightens. "It's okay. It's okay."

"How about we get out of here?" one of the other women asks. "They've already tried to kill us once, and we've found Roze. Let's go."

The other one squeaks an affirmative.

Reluctantly, Dovana and I finally pull apart, our gazes still lingering on each other. That's not a great sign. "Okay. Let's go someplace else, and we can discuss everything," I say, hoping by then I'll know what to say.

Dovana nods and grins as we weave back through the crowd. Fortunately, no one else tries to eat them—maybe because they're with me—and we make it outside. "Let's not stay out here any longer than we have to," Dovana says. "I don't think they liked us. Let's go back to the dorm. This is Caroline, by the way, and this is Taya." She points to the brunette and the black-haired one.

I manage to tear my gaze away from Dovana enough to properly face them. "It's nice to meet you."

"Likewise," Taya says.

Caroline nods.

"Okay. Fine, I'd rather not be out in the middle of the city anyway."

Taya offers me her jacket so I can pull the hood over my head to avoid attracting attention, and we hurry back to Dovana's dorm room, not taking the time to talk lest we be overheard. And now, after I've been avoiding it since I was six years old, I'm finally in Dovana's home with her. I finally accepted her invitation.

CHAPTER SEVENTEEN

DOVANA

She's really here. Gulping, I stare at the one-eyed woman sitting on my bed, her messy light blond hair framing her angular face. She's not quite how I'd pictured her. I'm not sure what I expected. I didn't imagine her as a little girl anymore, but I never thought she'd be so, well, beautiful. If I was less exhausted, I might be blushing at that.

Instead, my heart is still racing a mile a minute. We were almost eaten. I almost got Taya and Caroline killed. At least I wouldn't have had to live with myself, but that's hardly an excuse. I'm gonna have to talk with my ethics professor.

I clear my throat, trying to force myself to say something, but what? It's been fifteen years, and I still don't even know what I want to say.

Roze offers a faint, hesitant smile, emphasizing her striking cheekbones. "Are you all right?"

I stare at my feet. "I think so."

"No," Caroline shouts. "They were going to eat us!"

"They didn't," Taya says.

"I'm sorry," I mutter.

Caroline reaches across Taya, taking my hand. We're all sitting on her bed, save for Roze. I'm not sure how we ended up like this. I kind of want to go over to her, but I'm scared. I don't know what to make of any of this just yet. "I'm not blaming you. I wanted to help. I just didn't realize what I was getting myself into."

"But we found her," Taya says.

"We did. But how?" I ask.

Roze's smile turns into a grimace. "I was looking for you."

"What?"

She folds her arms around her belly, pressing the white dress close enough to show how thin she is. "I felt something was wrong. It was like nothing I've ever felt before, and I couldn't ignore it. It kept dragging me back to Toronto. It was practically screaming."

"I don't understand."

Roze nods, her brow knitting as she looks at the hardwood floor. "And I'm not sure how to explain it. It's like how I know when children are in danger but different, and it pulled me right to you."

"You know when kids are in danger?" Caroline asks. "That's a weirdly specific power."

Taya leans in, peering at her. "Can you detect every child in trouble in the whole world?"

She shakes her head. "No. It doesn't work like that. I simply know when there's a child in the woods who needs my help. It's how I met our mutual friend." Roze shoots me a hesitant smile.

"Is that how it works?" I ask. "You've mentioned it some, but I never really understood it. I thought it was like a Spidey-sense."

"What's a Spidey-sense?"

"Spider-Man?" Taya offers.

She cocks her head.

"Okay, then."

"Am I missing something? Was he one of the monsters there?"

Caroline laughs. And laughs. And keeps laughing to the point where she sounds like she's hurting.

"Are you okay?" I ask.

She coughs, shaking, still laughing. "I'm fine," she says, her eyes watering.

We all stare at her.

"I think it's the adrenaline."

Taya stands up, gesturing at the bed. "Do you need to lie down?"

She shakes her head.

"Are you sure?"

"I'm sure. Thank you."

"I'll happily offer your own bed to you anytime."

Caroline rolls her eyes but isn't shaking anymore. Maybe Taya's joke was so bad that it finally stopped her laughing.

Taya takes her seat again, peering into my friend's eye. I can see how badly she wants to comment on it, but fortunately, she apparently has some restraint. "Thank you. For saving us."

"It was no trouble," Roze says.

"Your English is really good."

"As is yours."

She blinks. "Okay. Fair enough."

Roze chuckles, seeming to relax the slightest bit before stiffening again. "Dovana convinced me to learn it since she was trying to work on hers and wanted to use it in our letters. It's been useful since a lot of children I've needed to help out of the country speak English."

"You just rescue children?"

She nods. "Of course. I'm a laume. It's what we do."

Taya shrugs. "That's so weird. But I guess not weirder than anything else."

Her brow crinkles. "What's weird about it?"

"Just, most people have jobs."

"I'm not a person."

Holding up her hands, Taya concedes the point. "I'm in so far over my head. A week ago, hell, three days ago, I'd have said that monsters aren't real. Now I'm talking to a fairy in my best friend's bedroom. Again."

"Taya," I shout.

Roze groans. "And now I have to grind your bones to flavor my food."

"What?"

Her clearly herbivore teeth show in a playful grin. "Just don't say it again, Ruskie."

"That's not actually a slur," I point out. "If you want to piss her off, call her a dirty commie."

Taya sits bolt upright. "Now wait a minute."

"A commie?" Roze asks. "What is a commie?"

"It's nothing," Taya snaps back.

Caroline chuckles.

"No laughing," Taya shouts. "You'll send yourself into another fit."

She only laughs harder.

I roll my eyes. This is getting ridiculous. Maybe I should ask for some alone time with Roze? No, they've earned this, and they'd assume I was sleeping with her or something. And I'm not. "I still can't believe you're really here."

I swear she looks taken aback. Did I say the wrong thing? "I can't either," she says quietly. "I suppose I owe you something of an explanation."

"For why you've avoided me the last fifteen years?"

"I wasn't avoiding you."

"You talked about visiting people in your last letter. This is the first time you've ever been in my house." To my shock, the room blurs. I'm crying? I thought I was doing better than this. But I'm still hurt. Why wouldn't she want to see me? She's supposed to be my friend. But she just saved my life, so I can't even be angry at her. And that makes me even angrier.

Her jaw drops, and she stares at me. "I didn't even think...by Vaiva, that must have been awful. I'm sorry."

"But why, Roze?" I sniffle, doing my best to blink away tears. Goddamn it. This was supposed to be a happy reunion. I didn't mean to do this.

Caroline takes my hand again, and Taya wraps an arm around me, facing Roze on my behalf since I can't stop crying. "She's spent fifteen years trying to figure out why you weren't willing to see her. She'd even started to fear that you were a part of her imagination, and I didn't help there. You're supposed to be her best friend, yet she only hears from you once a year, and it's radio silence the rest of the time. And don't say what's a radio."

"I know what a radio is," she mumbles. Clearing her throat, she tries to look into my eyes, but between my tears and her only having one, we struggle. "I'm sorry, Dovana. I had my reasons."

"And what were they?" At first, I think Taya asked it, but when I find that I'm standing and have crossed halfway to her—which isn't saying much—I realize I'm the one who said it. "I was six. I'd just made a new friend, and then I turned around, and you were gone. My parents didn't know what to believe. At least until that gold showed up."

"But I did leave it. And I always have. Just like you leave me bread. We leave presents and letters for each other. That's what friends do."

I take a deep breath, staring. "Friends are honest with each other, Roze. Now tell me, why? What did I do wrong?"

"You didn't do anything."

"Then what?" I yell.

She flinches away, staring at my knees. "I had a vision."

"You what?"

"What are you talking about?" Caroline asks.

"She's psychic," I say, not daring to take my eyes off her lest she disappear all over again. "Laumes can have visions of the lives that children will grow up to have, and hers are exceptionally strong."

"It's not just for children. That's the norm, but those of us who have exceptionally strong visions can see more."

I nod. She's told me all of this before. "Well, what did you see?"

Roze hesitates, looking out the window.

She was just on the other side of it earlier this week, eating my cooking and drinking my mother's gira. I wonder if she's thinking the same thing. I take her hand, trying to reassure her. I'm scared and upset, and I need an explanation, but scaring her isn't going to help. "Please, Roze. Tell me."

"I…" She pulls her hand away, turning fully to the window. For a moment, I'm scared she'll walk right out it, but she doesn't take a step. "I shouldn't tell you. It will sound absurd."

"Why? I know you can see the future. It's not any weirder than anything else about you."

"It's not…I saw us getting married."

I blink. I stare. I blink again. I reach for her hand, then stop, shake my head, and stare at her more. "What?"

"Called it," Taya says. I hear a thump, and she adds, "Ow."

"It's why I ran. That sort of thing isn't allowed. It's not supposed to happen. And I was only six, and I saw our entire life. I've never been in a vision before. It only works on humans. But I saw us walking down the aisle. I saw us living together. Every time I've tried to talk to you, tried to convince myself that I've changed it, I see it again. Sometimes, things are a little changed. We live somewhere else, or you have a different job, or your hair is different. Sometimes it's that minor, but it never really changes. You mean so much to me. You're my best friend. But I had to try to change it. I couldn't do that to my people, and yet, nothing seemed to make a difference."

I fight back more tears. She really has been avoiding me. And we were going to get married? We barely know each other. And she claims she cares despite having been avoiding me. Now I'm just repeating myself. This doesn't make any sense. "I don't understand."

"I can't let my people die out. We have to breed. We have to find someone else to make a child with. And I certainly couldn't do that with you."

"No, I know all of that. Though it also raises its own issues, but I'm not gonna touch those right now." I blow out a breath. I always retreat into philosophy. It's better than contemplating the mix of emotions in me at this idea. I want to examine the ethics of that system and what it would mean and what she'd really have to do, but it's not the point. "Aren't you straight?"

"I don't understand."

"That's my line."

She cocks her head. "Maybe I don't know the English word?"

I try again in Lithuanian because, of course, this is the only time we'd have this issue.

"Oh. I thought straight meant like a line."

"It means both."

She shrugs. "It is not quite the same for us. Laumes do not seek out relationships with other species, or at least it's very rare. We only use them for breeding."

"So you are gay?"

"Again, that's not really a meaningful distinction."

"Right." I always assumed she was straight. I don't think I would've been interested in her or anything, or apparently, I actually would have. Wow, it's weird thinking that my whole life is mapped out like that. And I never even got to know. "It was my future too," I find myself saying. What exactly is my point? I didn't want it. I'm not interested in her. Right? I think. I never really had the chance to find out. "Why do you get to decide for the both of us?"

She blinks. Or possibly winks, but I assume blinks. "What do you mean?"

That's what I want to know. What do I mean? "It was our future. You should've told me."

"I couldn't. I...if I..." Tears pool in the corners of her eye as she finally turns to me. "Dovana, I was terrified of what this would mean for my family."

"And you've had fifteen years to do something about that. You should've told me at some point."

She nods. "I'm sorry."

"And you know we could have just not gotten together." I can't even imagine being with her. "That seems like a pretty easy destiny to change." It's such a weird idea. No matter how amazing she looks all grown-up.

"You'd think." She holds her hands up as if showing off all the different ways she's tried. "I've done everything I could to change it. I've asked everyone I know."

"So, what, we're just meant to be?"

"Apparently."

"Aw," Caroline says.

"Oh, so *you* can give commentary," Taya mutters.

I turn to them as calmly as I can manage. "Shut up."

"I was not expecting this conversation to have an audience. Though I suppose I wasn't expecting this conversation to ever happen."

What? "You were never going to tell me?"

She gulps, turning away again. "Dovana…"

"You were just going to let me assume that you didn't want to see me? Forever?"

She takes in a sharp breath, wrapping her arms about herself. "I've been trying so hard, for so long, not to let what I saw come true. I didn't think about how it might make you feel. I know I've already said it, but I'm sorry. I'm not willing to be responsible for hurrying along the extinction of my entire species. There are not many of us, and if I wasn't going to have a child…I knew I couldn't do it, no matter what. Ever since I was a child, I knew that I had to find someone I could reproduce with and that it obviously couldn't be you."

"And have you not reexamined how insane that sounds since you were six?"

"It's not insane."

"Well, for starters, it assumes I'm going to fall in love with you."

"I'm not assuming it. I saw it."

I grit my teeth. Okay. She has a point there. I know how accurate her prophecies can be. One time, she said in a letter to make sure I left for school early on February fourth the following year. I almost forgot and was almost hit by a car on the exact cross street she'd mentioned. If it'd been even a minute later, I might be dead.

Though that would've saved her from marrying me. "And the rest of it isn't insane? Putting the entire survival of your race on your shoulders? Assuming that if I was to marry you—and that's a big if—that I wouldn't be okay with raising a laume kid? Apparently, that's how most laumes work anyway. How does that fear even make sense?"

"Because you're not a laume, Dovana. I shouldn't even consider having a life with you. You're just supposed to be my friend. That's all I wanted. And instead, when I was meeting the first human I'd ever known, the one who managed to convince me that they're not scary, I saw that I was going to betray my species and marry a human. Marry you. What the hell was I supposed to do with that?"

"Maybe talk to your best friend about it?"

"I can't."

"And why the hell not?"

"Because that's what leads to it," she shouts, tears streaming down her cheeks. "Half the times I've tried to change it, when I look again, that's the very occurrence that starts it. And I can't do it. I can't. And I won't."

"Roze—"

"No. I'm glad you're safe. But I will not do this to either of us. I'm leaving."

"No. Please." I reach for her hand only for her to pull it away. "I finally get to see you again. Please. I don't want to lose you."

She shakes her head, turning to the door. "I'm not doing this. I won't allow myself to." And she just walks on out. I don't even move to stop her. Not like I could anyway. What the hell do I do with any of this?

Chapter Eighteen

Roze

Tears stream unbidden down my cheeks. This was stupid. Obviously, I couldn't leave her to be eaten, but what the hell am I doing? I know this is how it starts, and I just went and did it anyway? I refuse to let destiny control me. I have a duty to my people, and I will fulfill it, and none of that involves falling in love with a human. No matter how beautiful she looks now. And she really does.

I shake my head. Vaiva, this is ridiculous. I won't let myself be distracted like this.

Wiping the tears away, I try to focus on anything else. If only there was a child in need of rescue. Hell, I'd take a house in need of cleaning, but nothing is calling to me. I need to take my mind off this. I can't just wait in her hallway.

Perhaps I should return to the place where I found her while I collect my thoughts. I don't need to worry about people seeing me there. Standing in the middle of this building crying with my one big eye isn't going to go over well, and I've no desire to handle people seeing me.

So fine. That crowded building. I'll head there.

I take a deep breath and walk right through the wall. It might not be the woods, but it's still a house, and we're as part of that as anything else.

Back outside, I breathe in the cool night air. There are people out, but I'm still wearing—was it Taya's—jacket, so I hide under the hood, stuff my hands in its pockets, and walk on, ignoring everyone and everything.

Why did my senses work for her? That's never happened before. Even people that I've saved before shouldn't trigger it; that only happens for endangered children. Is it simply because she was in enough danger? If I was brought to rescue her, then how was she only just in danger when I got there? Was I brought over because she was in a dangerous place? Or because she was looking for me?

I don't understand. Please say this isn't because I'm meant to be with her. I refuse to accept such a thing. I'm sure it's only a weird quirk of having saved her before, even if I have saved other people who later died, but that doesn't prove anything.

There's that weirdly small building. It's gray and nondescript, with only an incredibly unsubtle sign to distinguish it. Why am I even here?

Well, why not? I don't have anything more important to do, and maybe it'll help. I doubt anyone there can help with my fate, but if I don't find anything useful, at least it'll take my mind off Dovana. I prepare myself for that crowd and head on inside. I hope I didn't piss off anyone earlier.

The crowd is interesting. There are horns, wings, tails, any number of eyes, and any color of skin. I've never seen anything like it. In Lithuania, we're much more segregated. I wonder if this is the norm in Canada or if this place is particularly unusual even here.

"Hey there," a voice calls to my right. I turn to find a young man with horns and a long, coiled tail standing behind a table with a deck of cards on it. "Would you like your fortune read?"

Despite myself, I laugh.

His eyes flicker with annoyance and possibly, actual fire.

"I'm sorry. I've had a little too much of seeing the future. All it ever causes me is trouble."

"Maybe you're not looking at it the right way." He flips a card from the top of the deck, holding it out with a flourish. "The hanged man, inverted," he says without even glancing at it. "You're wrestling with an important decision, resisting what you know to be true, and wasting time here to avoid it."

"I don't need a card to tell me that," I mutter.

With an amused chuckle, he flips over two more cards from the deck, letting them fall on the table. The nine of swords and another nine of swords but upside down.

"Do you have two decks in there?"

"I suppose you could look at it that way." He smirks, clearly trying to give the impression that he knows more than he's letting on. He only wants my money. Not that it would cost me anything. "Turmoil, secrets, anxiety, and worry. It seems you're in dire need of some sage advice. I'm more than happy to provide it."

"You don't exactly look like a sage."

"I'm the closest you'll find around here." He gives me a smoldering look...literally. "I assure you, my prices are quite reasonable." His tail flicks forward, sliding a chair out for me.

"I really don't need it. I can see the future."

"And you've no idea what to do about it."

"I know perfectly well what to do," I say. And I'm doing it. I'm leaving her alone, just like I have to. It's what's necessary.

He gestures to the seat.

"This is a waste of time."

"But you're trying to waste time. So have a seat, pay up, and I'll give you the advice you clearly need."

For some reason, I don't walk off. I stare at the chair, trying to think of any good reason not to do this. I want to take my mind off of Dovana, and this won't help, but if there's something useful he can tell me...oh, fuck it. "Fine." Grumbling, I take the seat and hold out my hand, letting a meager helping of gold coins fall onto his table.

He stares at the pile.

"Is that not enough?"

He tugs on his black tie, adjusts the matching jacket, and feigns a smile. "Just caught me by surprise. That's all." He pockets the coins, his smile turning genuine as he lays the cards before him in a wedge with one at the top and three on either side of it going back toward me. "What is it that you'd like to know?"

I snort. "Shouldn't you already know that?"

He rolls his eyes—I think—they're a solid red, so it'd hard to tell. "Would you prefer I just tell you what the cards want you to know? Why the skepticism? It's not as if you don't believe in fate."

"And why would you say that?"

"As you said, you can see the future."

Right. Dumb question. Why am I being difficult? I already paid, so I might as well go along with this. "What do the cards want to tell me? How can cards even want things?"

He flashes another smile. "I don't think I can answer that second question, but the first, that's easy." He flips over the card closest to him, revealing an image of two blond women holding drinking glasses. It's stylized, but it looks like one of them only has one eye. That's unnerving. His smile only deepens. "The two of cups. It seems your problem has to do with love. Or at least a relationship, if you're not prepared to call it that."

"I'm not in a relationship." I'd sound more convincing if that card hadn't rattled me so much. How did he do that?

"Is that so?"

"Yes. It is so. Your cards clearly don't know what they're talking about. And aren't you supposed to deal them faceup, anyway?"

He rests his hand on the card to my left. "Ah, but that loses the drama. Perhaps I spent too much time in casinos, but I could never stomach not having the reveal." And with that, he turns a second card over, the overly dramatic bastard. Did he use these skills for cheating at cards? Does he use his magic to make them? How does he know so much about my situation?

I shake my head and look at the new card. The image is of a young woman—presumably me—with a broom. At least this one is a little less on the nose.

"You met her when you first started working."

"What?" Seriously, is he actually getting this from the cards, or is it something else?

"This card speaks of your past. You apprenticed to another laume—your mother, I'd assume—and in doing that, you found the object of your affections."

"She isn't—"

He waves his hand, silencing me and turning the next card. A cloaked figure sits astride a horse, the sockets of his skull showing under his hood and his hand reaching toward the one-eyed blonde. I shudder involuntarily and clear my throat.

"What does that mean?" It says "Death," as clear as day, but it can't mean that I'm going to die. Unless it's a threat? Did that guy from earlier set this up? He did seem somewhat demonic. Perhaps they're friends. If I had any sense, I'd leave or fight or at least take some action, but I just stare at the demon, waiting for an answer and hoping that it's less horrifying than I expect.

"It doesn't mean what you think. This card is about your present, and no, you're not about to die, at least, I wouldn't think so. I suppose one never really knows. But as this is about your relationship, and I assume she's not planning on killing you, this is about the change altering your life. Her."

"Nothing's changing." I grit my teeth, meeting his eyes. "Except that I'm not going to see her anymore."

"That would certainly be a romantic change. It could mean that."

I blink. I was sure he would argue with me. That doesn't mean…it couldn't…have I changed my destiny? Finally? Closing my eye, I try to concentrate on Dovana, on her future, and what it will bring. The vision is as it always is but missing the first step now that I've taken it. She and I talk at her parents' place, I apologize, and she forgives me, and then we start dating. Before long, we're married, and I have no way to continue my lineage. I still don't see a child, nor do I see any reason I would change my mind. It always ends at the wedding. My fist slams onto the table, and I stare at it. I hadn't meant to do that.

"The vision not to your liking?" he asks. "Perhaps I can change it."

"And how would you do that?"

"If it's a baby you're after—"

"What, you're offering?"

His eyes flash. "I can certainly think of a worse way to spend the night."

My skin crawls. I know I have to, but the idea has always made me feel sick. Maybe that's why I keep struggling with this.

It's not Dovana. It isn't how she makes me laugh or how passionate she is about everything in her life or even that she manages to make me care about things I shouldn't be at all interested in. Perhaps the reason I can't bring myself to change the future is because I don't want what's expected of me. Tears pool in my eye, and I blink them away. "Sure," I say, my voice cracking. "We should do that."

A hand rests on my chin, those red eyes boring into mine. "And what do you take me for?" There's something in his voice. Not anger but indignation. I didn't know demons could feel that. "I can see plain as day in the cards that I'm not the one you desire. My ego could never take spending the night with someone who wasn't into it."

I gulp, nodding.

"Would you like to see what to expect out of your Dovana?"

My eyes narrow. "I didn't say her name."

"Did you not?" He smirks, his too-perfect features looking all the more sinister. "Then how did I know it?"

"That's what I'm wondering." I glare, trying to look as intimidating as a being who's made primarily for housework and the care of children can be. Laumes aren't known for our warfare.

He laughs, and it sounds almost like an orchestra. "You don't need to worry. I'm not after anything. You already gave me gold."

"Then why?"

"It's fun. I love doing tarot readings." He gestures at the next card with its picture of the two women standing next to each other. Naked. The title "The Lovers" leaves even less to the imagination than their wardrobe. "This is your future."

"Not if I can help it." My voice is scarcely more than a whisper. All the conviction seems to be gone from it. Is this really all it took to sway me? A demon's parlor trick?

"And that takes us to the obstacle, doesn't it? Well, actually, it should take us to the other influences, but that's not as fun or dramatic." The new card is the woman—is Dovana—crying into her hands with nine swords on the wall behind her, but the card is facing him.

"Is that supposed to be upside down?"

The jab doesn't seem to faze him. "Well, it's hardly a good thing, if that's what you mean, but if you're asking if the card should be right side up, then no, they come precisely as they mean to." Why do I have a bad feeling about this? Oh, right, because he said it was bad. "As I'm sure you're aware, what's keeping you from your fate is your own inner turmoil and fears."

"Well, that's a waste of money."

"Like you care. It grows out of you." He studies the card, seeming to read something beyond the image. "The real issue, what's really stopping you, is your secrets."

"And what does that mean?"

"It means there's something you have to tell someone, and until you do that, you'll keep standing in your own way."

I grit my teeth, standing to leave. "I don't even know what I'm doing here. This is completely useless."

"I suspect you already know what I'm talking about."

"Well, I don't."

He shrugs. "Then you'll find out soon. The cards are for you, not for me. I can't tell you anything they don't say at face value."

"Then why am I even talking to you?"

"Is this how you treat everyone who tries to help you?"

I step forward, jabbing my finger at him. "Help? All you've done is con me out of some money."

"Roze—"

"And I didn't tell you my name," I shout. "I haven't told you anything, so where the hell are you getting all of this?"

He answers me with a soft smile. "We all have our skills, Roze. You can see the future, and while I have my own tricks to sort that out, I know love."

"What does a demon know about love?"

"That's some talk coming from a fairy."

"What did you—"

He holds out his hands. "Sorry. That was uncalled for. Much like several of your outbursts."

"What do you want?"

"Just to help. Name's James. I saw you in here with her earlier, and I could tell right away—"

"So you were watching me." I shake my head, turning around. It was all a trick. "I'm leaving. I don't know what I'm even doing here in the first place."

He sighs. "You don't want to finish your fortune?"

"No. I don't care anymore." I stomp off, hurrying out of the cramped building. I can't do this. I need to go home.

CHAPTER NINETEEN

DOVANA

I slump on the floor, staring at the door. "What the fuck?"

Caroline eases off the bed, sitting beside me and throwing her arm around my shoulders. "Are you okay?"

Still staring, I shake my head. "I don't know what I am."

"So did you know?" Taya asks. "Like, did you have any idea?"

"That I was prophesied to marry a laume? No. Can't say I did."

"Well good, that would've been awkward when we were dating. I'd hate to step on a fairy's toes."

I roll my eyes and shoot her a glare.

"There we go," she says, smirking like she'd won a gold medal.

"Yes, you're annoying enough to draw me out of my stupor. You're so talented."

"Thank you."

"Ugh." I groan, leaning back against the bed, the frame digging into my back. I don't even know what hurts the most. Her avoiding me, the fate that had been hidden from me, or her walking out again after all these years.

Caroline clears her throat, peering into my eyes. "Do you think you're interested in her? Like, would you even be willing to be with...someone like that?"

Another groan. "I never really thought of her that way. The last time we saw each other, we were kids." She did look gorgeous today, though. Not that it matters. And I definitely didn't notice how her dress clung to her ass when she walked out on me for good.

"She's kinda cute, if you're into that," Taya says.

"That's my future wife you're talking about," I say as jokingly as I can manage, but I still tear up in the process. Is she really gone? Am I not getting a letter next year? I don't care about the gold. I just don't want to lose my best friend. I blink away tears.

Taya, for her part, bites her tongue.

"Do you think she'll come back?" Caroline asks.

I shrug. "She didn't seem like it."

"She will," Taya says. "I'm sure of it. Hell, I thought you were a crazy bitch, and I still couldn't let you leave my life."

"But I kept trying."

"I wore you down. She'll be back, Vana. I know this is all scary and overwhelming, but you don't need to worry. Just deal with the whole prophecy thing, and worry about talking some sense into her later."

"But—"

"You can only handle one world shattering event at a time. I still remember when Griffith left A-Studio on the same day my father died. I really learned to prioritize. It's like triage. That's the term, right?"

"Yes. And you were twelve."

"Thirteen."

I sigh. "Okay, fine. I'm sure you were the only teenager in the world who knew how to effectively manage her emotions. That's very impressive."

"Yep. So focus on the one you can deal with. My father dying had been too much to process for a few days, but being sad about a pop band, I could manage. Do the same."

"You really focused on that when your father died?"

"I mostly focused on vodka, really."

"God, you're such a stereotype." I run my fingers through my hair, feeling almost ready to rip it out. Maybe she's right. I'm overwhelmed. I need to focus on one thing at a time. "So how does this work?"

Taya sits on the floor in front of me, her green eyes uncharacteristically sincere. "Since you were six years old, your fate has been decided, and no one bothered to tell you."

"God, it sounds even more fucked-up when you put it like that."

Caroline leans back. "I wonder if she could see my destiny."

"We can ask her when she comes back," Taya says. "How does that make you feel, Vana?

I purse my lips. There are so many emotions swirling about inside me right now. "Mostly? Pissed."

"Yeah?"

"She's been keeping this from me this whole time. I could've helped her solve it. We could've avoided it. Hell, we could've seen if we were even compatible in real life. But instead, someone who is supposed to be my friend has been avoiding me since our first meeting and has essentially been lying to me."

Caroline nods. "Yeah. It's a lie of omission."

"What else?"

"I can't believe it. I thought she was straight, for fuck's sake, and apparently, she even knew I was gay before I did. That would've saved me a lot of trouble if she'd told me. At least that part, if not that we were going to be together."

"Amen."

"She should've fucking told me."

Taya smiles. "She really should've."

"I don't understand why she didn't," Caroline says. "It seems like it would've only helped. You could've figured out what to do about it together."

"But instead, she has to do it all on her own. And hide it from me. And hide herself from me for fear of it coming true. I've assumed so many things over the years about her, and it all came back to this. If she'd just been open with me from the beginning, then who knows how different things could've been?"

"I'm sure it was scary for her too," Caroline says. "Had she ever even seen the future before?"

I chew my lip. She never said anything about visions when I first met her, but that doesn't mean much. "I don't know."

"Hey, she's the bad guy here," Taya says. "She can forgive her later."

"You're the one who insists she's coming back. And marrying her. We don't want her hating her wife before they even have their wedding."

"I'm not marrying anyone yet." I slam my hands into the floor.

"Sorry," they both say.

"It's not like she's even going to come back. I mean, I know you say she will, but she won't, really. Will she?"

Taya's damn smirk. "Apparently, you two are getting married, I think that sort of answers the question. She even said telling you like this was part of her vision. So apparently, you two make up."

"Huh." I blink. I hadn't even thought of that.

"You okay?" Caroline asks.

"It's kind of a relief, honestly. I don't think I could've handled losing her."

"We still don't know for sure."

"We do," Taya says.

Caroline glares at her. "Well, assuming that your ex isn't simply a crazy person, which I have never been quite convinced of, do you think you're okay with that future? I don't know what kind of life you can expect with a cyclops. She can't exactly go around Toronto without attracting attention."

"She could wear a veil."

I roll my eyes. "She's not gonna wear a veil. And clearly, she's had some way to manage. I mean, she's made it to my window all these years without ever getting caught. I think. I would've heard something. Right?"

"Of course you would've," Caroline says.

"You dodging the question, Vana?"

I shake my head. "No. I just…I don't know. I didn't ever think of her like that. She's very pretty."

"She is."

"Even with the…okay sure." Caroline holds up her hands, avoiding Taya's glare.

"But that doesn't mean I can marry her. I'm not in love with her. She's my friend. And she's not in love with me."

"Are you sure?" Taya asks.

I shrug.

Caroline says, "She wouldn't have been avoiding her all these years if she was."

"Or maybe that's precisely why she was."

"I don't know if that makes sense," I say. "Why would she be avoiding me if she was in love with me? She knew we'd get married, so she must've known I'd be capable of returning her feelings."

"Yeah, but she thought it would be wrong," Caroline says. "Maybe she's just homophobic or something. I didn't really understand her reasoning. But if she's too scared to love you, then that would make sense. Right?"

Taya gestures at her. "The straight girl has a point."

Pulling myself to my feet, I shake my head. "We can speculate all we want, but none of it gives me an answer."

"Then what are you going to do? Do you have some other way to learn about laumes? Because I don't think we can go back to that fiend place."

Sighing, I pull my phone from my pocket. "Well, I have one person I can try."

"Oh?"

"Maybe my mother would know something." It sounds even crazier now that I've said it aloud. She's not an expert or anything; she only lived in Lithuania for a lot longer than I did. And she had reason to learn. Or maybe I want to tell my mommy about how my fiancée dumped me. I type out a message before I can think better of it. *I know it's late, but I need to talk to you about something. Could you come pick me up?*

"I take it back," Taya says. "Trying to get eaten again was a better idea."

"Some of us have healthy relationships with our parents."

"Why?"

I sit back on my bed, shaking my head. "Because they're great. Now, unless we want to get bitched at by a pixie again, this is the best plan I have." And it gets me home cooking and someone who actually knows my relationship with Roze well enough to care. I won't have to explain everything to her. "So I'm going to see if she knows anything." God, why do I still sound like I'm investigating? I'm mourning now, and I know it.

"We could try the bread thing again," Caroline says, staring with tears in her eyes. She already knows I'm giving up, doesn't she?

"Do you have any more bread?" Taya asks.

I shake my head. "Maybe I'll see about getting some from my mama." And that's that. At least I have a plan, even if it's just crying in Mama's arms. Maybe Taya's right, but I have no way of knowing, and everything she said hurt. And they can't understand what I'm going through.

"Do you want me to go with you?" Caroline asks.

"It's fine."

"You could watch her make rude remarks at me," Taya says. "You love that."

"Now, that's actually tempting. But no. I just want to see her myself."

"Okay." Taya sounds so unsure, so worried about me. I guess she has reason to be.

Caroline asks, "Are you coming back tonight?"

"I don't know. Maybe."

"I could stay up. We could watch our show when you get home."

I shrug. I don't think Taya's idea worked. Maybe mine will.

CHAPTER TWENTY

ROZE

I don't even make it back to Lithuania before my mother finds me. She stands beneath a leafy tree, her arms crossed, and a cloven hoof tapping against a root. "Hi, Mother," I say. "Did you need something?" If she needs my help, then the whole business with Dovana will have to wait. Maybe there's someone to rescue. That would at least take my mind off everything.

"Don't be foolish, my dear child." She crosses the distance between us in two quick steps, resting her hand on my cheek.

"What?"

"You think I can't sense when my only daughter needs me? You ignored everything I said, didn't you?"

I take a step back, and it takes me a moment to figure out why the world is blurring again. "That hardly seems like helping."

She chuckles, her hand still on my cheek as if she teleported to keep trying to comfort me. But she's the one upsetting me. "You can hardly fault me for calling out my fool of a child on her foolishness."

I groan, not bothering to move away. It does feel kind of nice.

"We went over this a brief while ago. We shall die out, and it is not your fault, nor your burden to carry."

"But—"

"I will not watch my child deprive herself of the very happiness she's been ignoring all these years just so she can try to drag us out another generation. It will not change a thing. I'm only sorry that I didn't realize your secret earlier." With a heavy sigh, she pulls away and stares at the grass. "This is all my fault. I never made friends with those I saved, and all I ever wanted was to raise a child of my own, but I never meant for you to see that as the only option. If I'd understood why you were avoiding her…but I didn't even think you were avoiding anyone. You went far more out of your way to interact with her than I ever have for anyone."

"She's my friend."

A soft smile greets me as she turns back. "She's clearly more than that, but that is precisely what I mean. You care for her so much, and yet you think that you have to throw that all away. And that is my fault. I should not have raised you to believe so strongly in the importance of our survival. I never realized the strain that that would put on you."

"Mother—"

"Child." She pulls me into a tight hug, her head resting under my chin. "I'm sorry. I never meant to suggest that you shouldn't do what makes you happy."

I move back, staring at her, blinking away my tears. "I don't understand. We have to survive. You can't just change your mind on that because you want a daughter-in-law."

She chuckles, allowing the slightest bit of mirth into her dour expression. "We will not survive, no matter what we do. When I thought it was a thing you could stomach, of course I wanted you to carry on our traditions, but it was never a requirement, particularly not if it would make you unhappy. Tell me, Roze, can you truly see yourself lying beneath anyone other than Dovana?"

"Yes! I'm not in love with her."

"And yet you can see the future clear as day. I don't mean to ask if you're willing to…though I suspect we both know the answer to that."

"I…I." I hesitate. "I could. It's not like it would have to mean anything. It never does. I just have to make a child."

"It typically takes more than a single try."

I blink.

"Precisely. Now, my dear child, what do you see? Ignore the future you're avoiding, and tell me if there's any other. Let alone one where you'll be happy."

Taking a deep breath, I look at her hooves and the trodden grass and flowers. It's much easier to sort out the future when I have a specific person to investigate and much harder when that person is myself. The variables grow much more complicated. Before me, I no longer see the forest branching out in every direction. Instead, I see my future. I see dozens and dozens, if not hundreds, of ways for Dovana and I to fall in love. The path I'm on leads right to one, and it shines with a brilliant clarity.

Every other path leads to her as well. I search everywhere, just for the idea that I could find someone else, that I could move past her. I've tried it so many times, searching for a way to be free of her, of my fate, and yet the actions that would require of me are unthinkable. In no world can I turn my back on her. She's my best friend.

"If I stop speaking to her," I say, my conviction gone. It's simply not possible. We're meant to be.

"That wasn't the question."

I clear my throat, finding the tears have renewed themselves. "I just want to be good for our people. It's all I've ever wanted."

Another hug. I sink into it. "I know." Her fingers run through my hair as she murmurs comforting sounds. "But I'm telling you not to. This isn't your destiny despite your decisions. It's your destiny because of them. You want her in your life, and I don't want you to keep running."

I nod.

"If that's not what you want, then I'll see about finding someone for you. Simply give the word."

"But I'm not in love with her yet. How can I make a decision based on emotions I don't have?"

"You love her, even if you're not in love with her. Don't throw that away."

Tears run down my nose, but I ignore them. "Are you sure?"

"You can still have a child if you wish, but I'm not willing to do this to you."

"But what will it mean for Dovana?" I ask, as if I haven't already seen every possibility. It doesn't matter how much I tried not to look. I know the answer. I just don't want to be the one to give it.

With a heavy sigh, she pulls back, wipes her eye, and looks me up and down. "She'll come around, as long as you apologize to her."

I choke, strangling any reply. I can't bring myself to say a word, so I simply nod.

"And you won't harm her. The effects to a human are minor. If anything, she'll probably have a longer life."

"Are you sure?"

She seems to hesitate, but she meets my eye when she says, "I am. You saw it."

"I did."

"Then there's nothing to worry about. Go. Talk to her. Before she decides she doesn't want fate controlling her life and shuts you out for good."

"She won't."

"You know you're exhausting to advise." Her hand rests on her hip, but the scowl can't quite make it to her eye. "You can't look ahead to the answer for everything I tell you."

"Are you sure? Not that I can't look ahead, obviously I can, but are you sure this is the best option? I don't want to be responsible for the death of our entire species."

"You're not. We'll only make it a few more generations either way. Just don't go running off to live with humans and forget about us."

My jaw drops. How could she even think that? "I would never."

She squeezes my hand. "Of course. Then perhaps you can join me again soon. I did love tending that house with your help."

"Of course, Mother."

"Then hurry on. Go find your girl."

I never thought I'd hear her say that about Dovana, and no vision seemed to consider it worth mentioning. Perhaps even fate never thought I'd be this foolish. I'll not give myself any more time to question. I have to talk to her. I just hope she'll forgive me as easily as I've always seen.

Chapter Twenty-one

Dovana

"Hey, Mama," I say as I climb into the car. How am I going to explain all of this? "Do we have any Zalios Devynerios at home?"

"Wow, this really is important." She chuckles. "What happened?"

"But do you have it?"

She rolls her eyes. "Yes, we have it. God, I don't know how you can even stand that stuff. It tastes like NyQuil. And looks like it too."

We've had this conversation a million times so I play it up. My jaw drops, my hand flies to my heart, and I stare at her, as shocked as can be. "If you think that's what NyQuil tastes like, then I'm gonna go get a cold, and you can bring me all the NyQuil you can find. Because I will drain it."

"It just tastes like green."

"And I love the flavor of green. Red is good too."

She pulls the car out of the parking space. "We live in Canada now. You don't have to put yourself through that torture."

"You're right. I should put some maple syrup in it."

"Lord, what will I do with this child? She tries me so."

"Mama!"

She chuckles. "Can't you just drink Irish whiskey like a normal person?"

"Ah, that's so much more Canadian."

"It's still the west. We couldn't have that growing up in the Eastern Bloc."

Great. Way to take the fun out of it. I stick my tongue out at her. "You can't win every argument with Soviet oppression."

"I've made it this far doing so. I think I can manage a few more years."

"Why did I even call you?"

She pushes on my shoulder, giving me a quick smile and glance as we hit a red light. "But why did you text me? What's going on, my dear gift? Please. You never keep things from me. What's happened?"

"I need the alcoholic NyQuil in me first." It doesn't taste like NyQuil. She must've had too much whiskey on the way over. It's beyond delicious, but I have to keep referring to it like that all night or else, what's even the point?

"Oh, fine." She sighs. "Then what will we talk about? Have your classes been going all right?"

I've barely even paid attention to them this week. I probably shouldn't tell my mom that. "It's been pretty good. I'm a little behind on the reading, but I think I understand it pretty well. It just takes some work. Foucault is not the most concise person. It is really interesting working with a more contemporary philosopher, though. Other than the existentialists, I haven't really had the chance for that before. Though he still studied under them and was even French. Wow, there are a lot of influential twentieth century French philosophers."

"Right," my mother says, glancing at me as if she has no idea what I'm talking about. She never did quite understand my interest in the subject.

"Did you read that book I gave you? I really think you'd like Kierkegaard if you gave him more of a chance."

"I read through the first page about ten times before I had to take some aspirin."

"It's not that bad. I bet Roze didn't have that much trouble with it." My stomach churns at the mention of her name. Great, why did

I have to think of her now? "Maybe you just don't actually know English that well."

"I think once I started saying hair, singular, instead of hairs, I finally had a grasp of the language, but you bought it in Lithuanian, remember?"

I stare at her. "Oh. Right." How did I think to buy it for my mother in the right language and then only recommend the book to Roze? I should've at least grabbed a copy for her, preferably in the right language. Would she even be able to find one? Maybe I didn't think it'd fit on the windowsill.

"I'm glad my daughter is so much smarter than I am."

"Mama, you have a doctorate in physics from Vilnius University. You're not dumb."

"Then I'm just not a philosopher."

"You know physics was invented by Aristotle, so really, you still studied philosophy."

"I somehow now understand less about physics."

A laugh bubbles up, unbidden, and I can't keep from grinning. She gives me a playful wink before turning her attention back to the road. I am way too miserable to be this happy. "Is there any dinner left over?"

She shakes her head. "Sorry, Matis was really hungry. And so was your father. Did you not eat?"

"No, I did. It's just been a really crazy night."

"Do you want to stop for something? I'd know more what to say if you'd just tell me."

"Tim Hortons?"

"Wow, you really have gone native."

I roll my eyes. "I've lived here for over half my life. I think it's a bit late to say that."

"I could go for a coffee anyway."

She takes the exit a few before home, pulling into the Tim Hortons right off the highway. We get a couple coffees, some Timbits, and a sandwich. "I'm hungrier than I thought I was," she says by way of explanation for that last bit. "I'll split it with you."

"Sounds great."

It only takes a few more minutes to make it home. The house is totally silent. Even Matis must be asleep. I didn't know it was even possible for that brat to go to bed early.

Mama grabs a few bottles from over the stove and sets them and some glasses on the table, taking a seat behind them. "All right. So now you'll tell me?"

I pour a massive glass of Devynerios, drain it, and pour myself another. After a moment's hesitation, I empty that one as well.

"Wow," my mother says. "It's really that bad?"

Despite myself, tears stream down my cheeks. I try to clear the world, blinking repeatedly, and stuff a Timbit into my mouth. "It is."

"Is it something to do with Taya? Did she get a new girlfriend?"

I shake my head. "I'd be happy for her. Mostly. I mean, I'm sure I'd be a little jealous, there's still something there, but we're just friends now. She can get someone if she wants. She can."

"Okay." She doesn't sound like she believes me. "Then, what is it? Something didn't happen in your search, did it? Oh God, and I've been being so flippant. Were you mugged? I told you not to go downtown. Vana, tell me you're okay."

I shake my head. "Roze…" I don't even know how to go on. Do I start with the search? Can I even manage to stop blubbering long enough to talk about it? I sniffle, snorting, and help myself to another shot.

My mother stares. "But that was a few days ago. Are you just now telling me?"

I shake my head. "No. I saw her. Tonight."

Her eyes widen. "You found her?"

"In her letter, she mentioned visiting other people, so when I realized she could come see me, I needed to know how to contact her so that we could hang out. Or just actually get to see each other's faces for the first time in decades. I was worried she wouldn't want to, but I tried not to let myself believe that. So I started looking around, talked to an Irish fair one…he was a complete asshole."

"Of course he was." She nods sagely and takes a sip of whiskey.

"But he told me about this place where all the monsters—well, fiends, apparently—in town hang out. He wasn't sure where it was, so Taya, Caroline, and I started looking."

"You've been out there more than just today? Why didn't you tell me before?"

I shrug.

She stares at me, unblinking. "But you tell me everything."

"Sorry."

"Dovana—"

"It wasn't anything like that. I just didn't think about it. I'm sorry."

"Okay," she says, sounding unsure.

"But we found the place."

"You did?"

Nodding, I continue. "She wasn't there, but lots of other fiends were. One of them took an interest in us."

"What happened? Are you okay?"

"He only wanted to sell us as slaves. Or maybe eat us. I'm not entirely sure."

"What?" She slams the glass down, pushing it away, then she seems to reconsider and drinks the whole thing before pouring herself another.

"It was fine. Roze rescued us."

"You really saw her?"

"I told you I did." I smirk, but it quickly falls away. "But when we got back to my dorm..." I hesitate. "She told me about our destiny." How the hell am I going to explain this?

"What?"

I chew nervously on a doughnut hole. "You know how laumes can see the future?"

"Yes, of course. And you've said before that Roze is uniquely talented at it."

"She is." I sigh. "And apparently, when she and I met, she saw a vision for me. Well, for us."

"Our family?"

I shake my head. "No. Her and me."

"Oh." Understanding crosses her face.

I close my eyes, the tears picking up again. I don't know what I want. All I know is that it hurts. "And she didn't want it. She's been avoiding me this entire time. She's supposed to be my friend, and instead, she's been refusing to be near me. Just because she saw that we were going to get married, and apparently, that idea so repulsed her that she'd rather never see me in person again. It took almost being eaten—"

"You said it was nothing to worry about!"

All I can manage is a shrug.

"I'm so sorry, my gift." She rounds the table and wraps her arms around me, pressing my head to her chest. "That's the worst decision she's ever made. You're wonderful. You're too good for her. If she doesn't want you, then you'll find someone even better. Someone with depth perception."

A pained chuckle escapes my lips. "It's never seemed to affect her. Not that I've ever had the chance to see for myself."

"Do you want me to talk to your grandmother? I bet she knows what hurts laumes."

"I don't want to hurt her."

"I think it's iron."

I consider that. It would be so easy to prick her with some nails…if I ever see her again. She hurt me, she took away my agency in my own life and deprived me of my best friend, and it's so very tempting to pay her back in kind. But I saw how scared she was. I'm not the only one hurting. "No. I really don't want to hurt her. I want to have her in my life. Not like that seems to be an option." I wipe my eyes. "I can't believe she's really gone."

"Are you sure she's gone? What did she say exactly?"

"I don't know, but it was something to the effect of, I can't stop this prophecy from happening if I keep interacting with you, so I'm going to stop, good-bye forever."

Her hug tightens, squeezing the air from my lungs. She rests her chin on my head. "I'm so sorry."

I shrug.

"Do you want me to make you something? Potato pancakes? Gira? It will take a few hours, but I'll do it."

I shake my head.

"Dovana—"

"I'm okay."

"Are you?"

Well, great, she wants me to actually be honest. "No. I'm not. She means the world to me. And now she's just gone." She walked out. She doesn't want anything to do with me. I might not even get a letter next year.

"I'm sorry."

I blink away more tears. "I'm angry at her. I want to throw a handful of nails in her face, but I also miss her already and want to hold her and talk to her and finally spend time with my oldest friend. And I can't. And it's ridiculous. And it makes me hate her a little, and then I go back to the nail idea."

"I understand." She pulls away, and I miss her embrace. She grabs the bottle of Devynerios and tops off my drink before taking a sip of coffee. "I'm here for you."

"I know you are. Thank you, Mama."

"Always, my dear gift."

I empty my glass and shovel some doughnuts in my mouth, then follow them up with even more booze. That's starting to make me feel a little better. My head swims, but only a little. I'm Lithuanian, not some lightweight Canadian girl.

She chews on a Timbit as she looks pensively at me.

"What're you thinking?" I ask.

"That I want to beat her up for doing this to you. But also, that we should try talking to her."

"How? And she won't listen anyway."

"Do you think she might just be scared?"

With an annoyed groan, I nod. "I'm sure she is. Having your future chosen like that must be terrifying. Hell, it's terrifying for me twice over. I found out that I have this whole future where I end up married to a beautiful fair girl, and then someone else chooses for me to not have that. Both were decided without me, and I just have to deal with it. I hate it. It makes me feel like I'm some plaything with no willpower of my own. Nietzsche would be disappointed. And so would his mustache."

"What?"

"I'm pretty sure his mustache has a will to power all on its own."

"How much have you had?"

I pour another glass. "Not enough."

"Just don't die of alcohol poisoning under my roof."

"I'll go outside."

She chortles. She must've had a bit too much to drink herself. "Thank you. That's all I can ask."

I pour her whiskey.

"Well, if you insist." She sighs and quickly chugs the thing. "Damn, that's good. So much better than your shitty NyQuil."

I roll my eyes.

"Can you try setting bread out?"

Footsteps sound upstairs. "No. I tried that. It only got me that pixie."

"Maybe it will get her this time?"

"I think she'd have to choose it. And she's avoiding me, so there's no reason she would."

"Right." She sips as she weighs the situation. "We could go back home and march into the woods and give her a piece of our mind."

I can't help but smile. "Now, that's tempting. That may be the best plan we've come up with yet."

The stairs creak. "Dovana?" Matis's grating little voice sounds from the living room. "What are you doing here? It's Saturday."

I groan. "Hey, Matis."

"That's not an answer."

After some more alcohol, I nod, confirming that it was not, in fact, an answer. "Adult problems. Nothing you need to worry about. Go back to bed."

"It's the weekend. I haven't gone to bed yet. I was just on my computer."

"Then go back to your porn."

"Dovana," our mother hisses.

His face goes red. "I wasn't! I don't!"

I snort. "Well—"

A hesitant knock sounds at the door to the backyard. It's so quiet, I think it must be my imagination, but when I turn, there's a pitiful cyclops on the other side. "Roze?"

"Is that her?" Matis asks. "Wow. She's hot."

"Apparently, that's my wife you're talking about."

"What?"

Mama chuckles. "God, what am I going to do with you two? Do you want me to get that?"

"No." I shake my head, clear my throat, and regret the last four drinks. I wash down a few Timbits with some coffee, fix my hair—although she can already see me, so I'm not sure what the point is—and march on over to the door.

CHAPTER TWENTY-TWO

ROZE

"Hi," I say with a pitiful little wave. What am I even doing here? Other than living out something I've been watching since I was six and spent decades trying to avoid. But here I am, still terrified but almost desperate for it to come true. A few minutes ago, I was throwing her away, and now I'm scared that I've lost her forever. What is wrong with me?

"Hi." She doesn't sound thrilled to see me. Her arms are crossed, and not only is she glaring at me, but her mother is too. I've seen her quite a few times before but never actually made her acquaintance. Part of me had hoped that I'd make a better impression, but I always knew it would come to this.

I clear my throat. That fails to accomplish anything, so I scratch my calf with my ankle and grind my heel on the lawn. None of it seems to clear the air, so I suppose I'll have to talk. I'm not even going to cheat and check the speech I'm supposed to give. I suppose it'll come naturally. "I'm sorry." That's not a speech. Damn it.

"You're sorry?" She takes a step, glaring straight into my eye. Her voice is low and as furious as her blue eyes. "You're sorry for lying to me my entire life? You're sorry for avoiding your best friend and then tossing her away like trash? Or are you sorry for showing up in my mother's backyard in the middle of the night? Oh, how about for how all of your secrets led to me almost being eaten?

Maybe you're just sorry for saving me from those woods in Babtai all those years ago. If I'd died, you wouldn't have had to deal with any of this, and you'd be much better off."

Her breath stinks of alcohol. I never smelled anything in the visions. I hadn't realized she'd be drunk for this conversation. That's going to make it less pleasant. "Yes. I'm sorry for all of...well, most of that. I'm not sorry I saved you. I am sorry I interrupted your time with your family."

"Oh, is that all?"

I shake my head, blinking away tears. "I shouldn't have hidden everything from you." My voice cracks saying it, and I let out a shaky breath. "You deserved to know as much as I did. I was scared. I was a child."

"And you haven't been a child for a good long while now. You had more than enough time to be honest with me, Roze. You've had years. But you didn't want me to know. Why, am I not your type? You found the idea of marrying me, of falling in love with me, all repulsive that you'd rather cut me out of your life?"

I screw my eye shut, pinching the bridge of my nose. I'm stupid. Every time, I see more and more how little I considered her feelings on this. Of course it would make her feel unwanted. "No. It seemed like a deed that would never be allowed. And more than that, laumes' destinies aren't supposed to be foreseen like that. That's a human thing. Having control of my life taken away like that terrified me."

"And you think it doesn't for us? I certainly had goals for my life. I thought I'd be choosing them, and instead, it's already been picked out. But then on top of that, I'm not even supposed to have that life? What do I get, Roze? My life is controlled, and I'm forbidden from going where it leads." The alcohol does nothing to slow her tongue. Perhaps she's simply angry enough that it carries her through it. She certainly looks it.

I want to argue that I felt the same way, but I lost the right to that argument when I hurt her. It doesn't matter how I felt when I took it all out on her. I was cruel. "I'm sorry."

"Yeah. You've said."

"Maybe you should go," her mother says.

"Do you want me to leave, Dovana? I will."

She grinds her teeth, staring at the grass. "Why are you here?" There's no curiosity or warmth in her voice. Only a cutting cold. I deserve that.

"To apologize—"

"Well, you've done that."

Saying I changed my mind sounds far worse. "I don't want to lose my friend."

"Sure could've fooled me. What happened to good-bye forever?"

I'm not sure I actually said those words. "My mother talked some sense into me. All I've been doing was hurting the both of us, and I'm tired of it. I've been holding myself up to this…" I swallow. I need to say it to sound sincere, but the idea of allowing my race to die out still hurts me. "Absurd notion that no one else around me seems to even care about. I was wrong. And I shouldn't have put you through that."

"Well, you've told her," her mother says.

"Mama." Dovana meets her eyes. They look exactly the same.

Her breath tosses her bangs. "Are you sure?"

"I want to at least hear her out."

"Fine. Come along, Matis. We're going upstairs."

"But I want to watch."

"Now." Her voice is lower, in a tone that brooks no argument.

I shift my weight from one leg to the other.

After a long moment, Dovana asks, "Do you want to come inside?"

"If you'd like."

"You're not all that comfortable inside, are you?"

"Oh, no, it's fine. Houses are part of where I belong as well. It's not like your yard is a forest. I can come inside."

She turns around and takes a seat, pouring more green liquid into her glass. She gestures at the chair her mother had been sitting in. "Do you want any?"

Rather than pacing around the kitchen the entire conversation, I take the seat. "I'm not sure. I've never had any before."

"You've never had Zalios Devynerios? You don't know what you're missing."

"I'm sure I don't. I've never had alcohol of any sort." I chuckle. Far too awkwardly.

Her eyes widen. "How?"

"It never came up. We don't have any, and the children I save certainly don't. Oh, actually, I think I have had wine. That's alcoholic, right?"

"Barely. No one offered you any vodka or anything when you saved their kid?"

I shake my head.

"Okay then." She smiles for a fraction of a second, but it disappears as pain takes her face again. She walks to a cabinet and grabs another glass, then pours a drink and slides it over to me. "Drink. You're too sober for how drunk I am."

I take a nervous sip. "It burns."

She glances out the window, at the yard I waited in for a good ten minutes while trying to work up the nerve.

"But it tastes great." I finish the glass and start coughing. My lungs hurt. "Yeah. I'd love some more." I have to force the words out.

She shrugs and pours me another drink, sipping her own as she studies me.

I finish it off, grimace, and try to turn it into a smile. "So good."

She rolls her eyes.

"I'm sorry."

"Yeah. You keep saying."

"But I really am. I never wanted to hurt you. And it seems like that's all I do. Everything I've done my whole life—"

"Roze, I am still far too angry at you to be up for pitying you."

I nod, but a few tears escape. "I'm sorry."

"Stop saying that."

"I've tried desperately to escape our destiny, and I never stopped to think about how you would feel. I thought being together with a human woman would be wrong. That I wouldn't be able to continue my species when we're already dying out and that my family would never approve."

"You still could've told me."

"But I was wrong. No, I wasn't simply wrong, I was projecting. My mother has never shown the slightest bit of judgment over these things. She's saved the daughters of gay women, tended their houses, and one of her sisters never even had a child, and she didn't say a mean word to her. I always assumed that she was thinking it because she'd taught me about how close we were to extinction and how important our survival was." I wipe my eye and pour a refill. I need its pain to help with my own. "But that was me. I spent so long dreading the idea of having to find a compatible man to have sex with. Hell, to me, they'd have all been basically Baubas."

Her jaw drops, and the glass nearly slips from her hand, but she manages to right it with the table and it doesn't spill. "Baubas is real?"

"He is. One of my sisters had a child with him."

"Wow."

"Yes. It was news to me as well."

"Wow," she repeats.

I manage a smile. She's kind of cute like this. "I'm not in love with you. Though that apparently will come soon." Less than a week. I should tell her. Keeping it from her is only proving that I haven't changed. "I'm not sure of the exact day, my vision was never so kind as to show a calendar or anything, but I think it's maybe five, six days from now."

She stares at the table. I'm not sure how to read her expression, but I push on.

"I focused on it so much. On what I'd have to do. And the horror of it, when no one else seemed remotely concerned, even if they had to sleep with the boogeyman himself. I probably should've taken it as a sign."

"So you're gay?"

"It's still not really a concept we have."

Dovana snorts. "Well, it sounds like you're a pretty clear lesbian."

"Maybe." I shrug. "I don't think that's the important part."

"Accepting yourself is pretty important."

"Fine, then, I'm a lesbian. Happy?"

She drains her glass. "Not especially."

"Well, I want to change that. I know I don't have the right to ask, but I want to stop hurting you. And I want you to be in my life."

She studies the glass for a long moment before finally looking at me. "You mean so much to me, Roze. You really hurt me, but if you won't do it again, then I don't want you out of my life either."

"Can we…I mean we will…Do you want to know where our first date is supposed to be?"

She nods.

"I can't walk with another person, so I can't take you to any of the places I'd like. There's a restaurant we go to that's full of monsters. I think it's at that place I found you. I'd always wondered, and now I suppose I know."

"Makes sense." She still seems very cold, distant.

"You look happy when we go. I only saw bits and pieces, but it seemed genuine. I want to see you that way."

She opens her mouth but closes it again, probably biting what I assume was a justifiably cruel remark. "So is there something you want to ask?"

I find a sudden lump in my throat and swallow it with the alcohol. "Right. Yes. Of course. I want to ask that. I need to."

"Well?"

I take a deep breath, letting it out slowly. "Can I take you out for dinner? Maybe tomorrow?"

"I was gonna get caught up on homework." It doesn't sound sincere. It's like she's looking for an excuse to say no. Perhaps I deserve that. No, I know I do.

"I think the place is open pretty late."

Her fingers dance on the table, and she avoids my gaze for a long moment. When she finally turns to me, some of that coldness seems to have vanished. "Yes. I think I would like that."

"Great. I'll pick you up at your dorm room? Say, eight o'clock?"

"Do you have a way to tell time?"

I blink. "No."

She breaks into a laugh, her smile finally lingering. "Gimme a minute. I think I have a couple watches in my room."

"Okay. Should I wait outside?"

"No. It's fine. Have some more Devynerios. Seems like you could use it."

I'm not sure I can handle more, but if it'll make her feel better, I try to finish my glass.

She heads off, and I hear voices upstairs. She's probably telling her mother how it went, but I don't want to eavesdrop. When she comes back down, she has a pink bracelet in her hand. "It was a gift from my grandmother."

"I'll take good care of it."

Another laugh. I really like her laugh. And her smile. "It's a cheap hunk of pink plastic. Don't worry about it. You can keep it. I was simply trying to justify why it's so ugly."

"I think it's nice."

"Then I'm glad it's yours. I'll see you tomorrow."

"Okay." I turn but stop partway to the door and look back to her. "You're not just doing this because you think you have to, right? I couldn't change our fate, but that doesn't mean you have to go along with it. If you don't want this—"

"I do. I think. I at least want to find out."

"Okay. Then until tomorrow."

"I'll see you then."

She approaches me, and we both stare at each other for a long moment. We've never actually said good-bye before. I hug her and am both pleased and surprised when she hugs back. I'm really doing this. Wow. It looks like I have my first date.

CHAPTER TWENTY-THREE

DOVANA

Caroline's alarm doesn't wake me up. My little brother stomping down the stairs does, however. Right. I'm home.

I rub the sleep from my eyes and check my phone only to discover that it's dead. Shit. What time is it? Groaning, I fling myself out of bed and find that I'm still dressed. The motion sends the room spinning, and pain shoots through my head. How much did I drink last night?

I hurry downstairs to check the clock in the living room and almost run into my mother. "Oh, you're up," she shouts, her words sending knives into my skull.

Clutching my head, I manage a nod. I think.

"I told you not to finish off that bottle."

That explains it. Fuck. "You're always right."

"Of course I am."

"But—"

"Just a minute," she says, firmly but not too loudly, thankfully. "Did you want a ride back to the dorm?"

"Yeah. I'll take the ride. Just ibuprofen first. Please."

Chuckling, she walks off, taking her time.

"Are you sick?" Matis asks.

"I will be," I mutter. I don't usually get nauseous, but I've been terrified about tonight. I think I might have drunk most of Mama's whiskey too.

He pokes my belly, and it takes all of my willpower not to hurl on him. It would serve him right, but I don't want to do that to the carpet.

Footsteps thud behind me, and I have to screw my eyes shut. "I brought you some water too. Make sure you drink the whole thing." A cold glass presses against my hand, and I take it, taking a sip before holding out a hand for the pills. Once I've gone through two glasses of water, I'm not sure I feel any better, but I at least don't feel worse. They both laugh as I wince.

I grit my teeth and glare. "You're both enjoying this too much. Did I tell you what happened, Mama?"

"You mean that you have a date with a hot fae girl tonight? No, I don't think you mentioned it."

I blink. "I called her hot?"

"A few times. No more than five."

My jaw drops. What? I mean, I guess she is. But I didn't think… do I already like her? But I was going to find out tonight if that was even a thing. I normally don't go around saying that kind of stuff. Though maybe I would if I drank more often. Maybe that's the real moral here. If I drink more, then I'll know my feelings better.

Mama rolls her eyes. "We can talk about this in the car. Are you ready?"

I don't think I'm going to vomit. "Yeah. Let's go."

We climb into the car, and I do my best to handle my newly discovered motion sickness. Tonight is gonna be fun.

Once I've vomited, showered, and vomited again, I feel a bit better. When I'm drying off and trying to decide what to wear, I hear keys turning in the door. Well, it's not like it'll be the first time Caroline sees my ass.

"Oh," she exclaims as she comes in. "You're here."

"And naked."

"Right." She turns around, facing the door. "Tell me when I can look. Did everything go okay?"

I slip on my panties and start to grab some jeans, then bite my lip as thoughts of the coming night filter in. I have no idea what I'm going to wear, but I have a date. I have a date with Roze. God, that's such a weird thought. I could've sworn she was straight. I'll have time later. Wait, did we even agree on a time? I clutch my head. Thinking is hard.

Fuck it, leggings and a T-shirt it is. I can get all dolled up when I'm nervous and fretting over myself later. "I'm decent."

She walks over, a gentle smile on her lips. "I'll believe that when you're not green. Are you going to throw up?"

"Probably."

"How much did you have to drink last night? What happened to all your claims of Lithuanians being immune to hangovers?"

"We..." I swallow down something I'd rather not mention. "Are. Normally. I just drank an absurd amount."

"Right."

"I'm fine."

"You don't look fine."

I force myself to stand up straight and give something in the general vicinity of a smile. "I'm fine. More than fine."

"Are you sure?" She squeezes my shoulder, her brown eyes so warm and caring. It's a shame she doesn't want kids; she'd be a great mother. "I know you were trying to hide how much it hurt last night. You weren't succeeding, if you were wondering."

"I wasn't wondering but thanks."

She smirks. "I'm here if you want to talk. You don't have to put on an act."

"I'm not putting on an act. Well, maybe a little, as this headache is killing me, but not about being happy. And scared. And excited. Is all that showing?"

Leaning in, she studies me. "It's mostly the headache and nausea, but what's exciting you?"

"I have a date with Roze." Wow, I really do sound excited. I thought the nervousness was stronger. I don't even know if I want this. Right? Or is this because I'm fulfilling my destiny? I really don't understand. I just know I like her, and that she's drop-dead gorgeous, and that single eye look really works for her. Damn, maybe we are destined to be. Well, I know we are, but maybe there's some validity to it because I never thought I'd be so horny for the fae.

She blinks, taking a step back. "I'm sorry, you what? Didn't she say she was never talking to you again? And that you couldn't be together? She couldn't even make it a whole night without you?"

Laughing and grinning so hard it hurts, I shake my head. "No. She couldn't. She showed up at my parents' place about halfway through the bottle of Devynerios."

"Is that that weird liquor you made me try? It tasted like NyQuil."

"No, it doesn't. Why does everyone keep saying that?"

"Probably 'cause it tastes like NyQuil."

I groan. "It tastes nothing like it, but that's not the point. I have a date. And I think I might really like the idea of getting together with her."

"Sure seems it. You're grinning with the hangover of the century."

I nod. A little too quickly. My stomach churns, and I have to rush to the bathroom. My homework is gonna be a bitch.

My fingers dance on the table. I normally love phenomenology, but I don't think I have any idea what I've written. Gah, if I didn't know any better, I'd think the feeling in my stomach was butterflies rather than a couple bottles of liquor.

Should I go find Taya after I finish this? I normally do. And I know she'd want to know, but I feel like she'll be a lot judgier about everything than Caroline was. She saw how much Roze hurt me yesterday, and I'm not sure that things being better now will be good enough for her. Which is pretty ironic for my ex who sent me into therapy.

This is a thing I know. I think. It's Kierkegaard. But it's not about Roze, and my head is still on fire.

I screw my eyes shut, trying to draw knowledge from somewhere in the back of my brain. I can do this. I've read two of his books back to front, and I did all the reading for the lessons. This should not be so difficult. If only a certain one-eyed beauty didn't seem to be occupying my mind. It's still weird thinking of her like that, but I can't stop.

Okay. I think I've got it. I start to type, stretching as far back in my mind as I can reach for the required knowledge. Any other day, I'd have been able to go on for hours and explain everything perfectly, but I manage only a brief synopsis and some clear definitions. At least it worked.

Now I just need to focus on this paper. Somehow.

❖

"What?" Taya asks.

I blow out a breath and lean back on the bench, gazing up at the cloudy sky. I knew she wouldn't take it well. "Roze asked me out."

"What?"

"She came over last night and apologized and asked me out."

"What?"

"Did I break you? Like, seriously, do you need to be restarted? I know I've pressed your 'on' button before, but where's your 'off' button?"

"I'm not broken. I just don't understand what the fuck you're thinking."

I shrug. "Cute girl?"

"She left you in tears, said she never wanted to see you, and then stormed out of your life. And you what, are just going to welcome her back with open legs?"

"It's not like that."

"The hell it isn't," she shouts. "What is it like, then, Vana? You been reading too many young adult romances and wanted to try it out for real?"

"She's not a vampire."

"Right, because a fairy is so much better."

"Don't call her that."

She rolls her eyes and fixes me with a glare. "You were sobbing on your floor because of what she did to you. Now she just waltzes back? For what? And don't forget, fairy gifts always come with strings attached. Just what do you think she's going to want this time?"

I glare back. "I said don't call her that."

"Maybe she's after a quick lay. You know how the myths always portray them. Your fairy wants to see what it's like being with a human."

Stomping, I stand, towering over her for what feels like the first time in my life. "You don't have to be happy for me. You don't even have to like her. But apparently, this is a thing that's going to happen—hell, supposedly, it's a thing that has to happen—and I'm okay with that. I think it could even be wonderful. So you have to accept that. And if you so much as dare disrespect her like that again—"

She stands to meet me, her hands in her jacket pocket as she leans down to glare into my eyes with a threatening huff. "What are you going to do?"

Folding my arms, I stomp again and hold my chin high. I hadn't thought that far ahead. "You don't want to know."

"Nothing is destined, Dovana. So what, she came to your parents' house last night and started telling you how you couldn't fight destiny, and you just had to date her? She's manipulating you, Dovana. You don't have to do it just because she says that you will. You're better than this."

"That's not what it was like. She came back, and she talked to me, and she explained all of the fears and doubts she's had her whole life, and how her internalized what, miscegephobia—kind of—kept her from admitting that this was even a thing she could want, let alone that she actually wanted it. And I mean, you saw her. She's gorgeous. And she's been my friend for, like, forever. I'm not doing this because of her prophecy. I'm doing it because a beautiful woman who I really love talking to asked me out. Her having already seen our future together is more of a proof of concept. It means that I know that I can do it. And yeah, it's going to raise some philosophical questions about free will that I'd love to tackle—and will, possibly in my final—but none of that changes the main point here. I want to do this."

She stares at my feet, and I swear I see a tear run down her cheek, but she turns away too quickly for me to be sure. "But she hurt you."

"You've hurt me too. Should I stop being your friend?"

"Probably." She sniffles and wipes at her eyes. She is really crying over this? "I...No, it's nothing."

"Taya, what? What possible explanation do you have for... no, you were being a bigoted asshole, but you weren't being unreasonable. I understand why you're scared. And I'll be cautious."

"It's not that. Well, it's not just that."

"Then what?"

She groans, finally turning, her eyes shimmering. She doesn't even bother to wipe the tears streaming down her cheeks. "I know I'm the one who fucked things up because I didn't believe you, and now I know that you were completely right, and I was being an asshole, but I...I..." She takes a deep breath, blinks away a few tears, and looks right into my eyes. "I always thought we'd end up back together."

My jaw drops, and my heart stops. Or at least, it feels like it does. I pick my jaw up off the floor, then start to say something and stop. "You did?" I finally ask after fighting with myself.

She nods.

"But you're dating someone."

She shrugs. "It's not that serious."

"But you're you."

"What's that supposed to mean?"

I search for words. "It seemed like you were fine sleeping around and finding other girls and stuff."

"I am. I just thought that eventually, that would change."

"So, what, I'm your backup plan, and you're sad you might be losing it?"

"No." She takes my hands. I only try to pull away for a moment. "And I love being your friend. I thought we still had something there, and that eventually, we'd see where it went."

"We already tried that, Taya."

"I know, but I thought we'd try again."

I sigh. "I don't want that."

"Oh."

Great, now I feel awful. "I'm sorry. You're my best friend, and you mean the world to me. And yes, the reason we broke up is because you didn't believe me about something that was important to me, but the reason I want you as just my friend is because we're perfect like this. I know you'll be there with me through thick and thin, and I..." This is gonna hurt her. "I just don't feel that way about you anymore."

"Oh," she repeats.

I plant a soft, chaste kiss on her cheek. "I'm sorry. You still mean a lot to me."

"I know. And I wasn't even trying to get back together now. It's the idea of you running off and getting married—"

"No one is getting married yet."

"Right. Yet."

I take a step back and have to rub my eyes to keep her in focus. Great, now I'm crying. I have a date in a few hours. "I don't know anything for sure, but she could quite literally be the one. You know, the person I'm meant to be with. And I really like her, and holy shit, her body does things to me. I owe it to myself to give this a shot. And if we do get married, then I need you there to support me and be my maid of honor. Please."

"I thought no one was getting married yet."

"We're not."

"Just in preparation then?"

I roll my eyes and rather un-daintily sniff back my runny nose. "My point is that I need you there. You're my best friend."

She takes my hand again, squeezing tight. "And I'll be there, Vana. Always."

"Good. You better be."

She nods and pulls away to wipe her eyes. "I will be. Just go get ready for your date."

"It's not for a couple hours. And I already picked out my clothes."

She groans and glares at me through tear-rimmed eyes. "Then buy me pizza to make me feel better."

I laugh so hard I snort. "Okay. I can do that."

We soothe our tears with cheese and carbs and try to focus on anything but what my impending date will mean. She's clearly already thought about it enough for one day. And I could use the distraction. Besides, I'll find out tonight.

Chapter Twenty-four

Roze

I knock on the door to Dovana's room and pick at the hem of my new dress. I spent all day sewing it. I thought it would take my mind off the date, but it only gave me more time to worry. Why didn't I just go through the window? I hate waiting in this hallway. People could see me.

Snippets of conversation filter out from the other side of the door. "Holy shit, she's here." I chuckle. "I honestly thought she'd chicken out." It's not Dovana. I think she said her name was Caroline. She has a point. Why am I here? Why have I not...was it, pigeoned out? Wow. I'm so worried I can't even remember what she just said. Maybe someone will call for help? I could just leave. I could save someone. Dovana couldn't be mad at me for running away then.

Is that what I want?

I know my future. I know this is what I'll want. But does that really mean that I want it now? That I can want it? I've let myself do this, I think I know how I feel, but how can I really be going through with it? An image of her from last night flashes in my mind. Her breathtaking blue eyes, reddened and puffy from hours of crying. The way she'd felt pressed against me.

Vaiva help me. I think I really do. I want this. I try knocking again. I'm so not ready to have someone come out into the hall, see me, and start a ruckus before we even have a chance to go have our date.

"You can answer the door." Even shouting, Dovana's voice is faint, like it's coming through another door. She must be in the bathroom.

"Fine." The door swings open, and I see the same mousy woman from before with the rectangular-rimmed glasses. "Hi." She plasters on a disingenuous smile.

"Hi. Caroline, right?" I return her smile in kind. "May I come in?" I glance to either side to emphasize my point. None of us want to have to deal with those consequences.

"Yes. Fine." She steps back and gestures for me to head in.

The door slams behind me as I stand awkwardly in the kitchen-hallway-foyer of the little dorm room. I'm not too used to houses or human dwellings in general, but this seems particularly cramped now that I have the time to examine it. "Hi." Right, I already said that.

"Hi," she replies. She seems even less enthused this time.

With a heavy sigh, I stare at the floor between us. I'm sure Vana has already given some sort of explanation, but I must still owe her friends something. I wonder if I could just give them gold until they forgive me. "I must apologize for my behavior yesterday."

"Oh?" She folds her arms but gives no other indication of what she may be feeling.

I nod. The truth will sound awful, but I can't lie to her. Besides, Dovana probably already told her. Vaiva, I'm lucky I'm not a western fae with their inability to lie. That sounds awful. I hear they also can't have children, so at least it would prevent my whole issue in the first place. Maybe it'd be worth it. Plus, I've heard good things about depth perception and wings.

Wow, I'm really procrastinating here. "I was a coward. I tried to run away from my future not because I didn't want it, but because I was afraid to want it, and in doing so, I hurt someone we both care greatly about. I've already apologized to her, though I'll gladly do so again, but I know how awful that must've been to see, so I'm sorry to you as well. Thank you for looking after her after what I did."

She shakes her head. "She wouldn't even let me know how hurt she was. She didn't act like everything was fine—I don't think she even could—but I thought she was doing a lot better than she was. I messed up there."

"Still less than I did."

She snorts, the faintest hint of a smile tugging at her dour expression. "I'll give you that."

Is there a thing people are supposed to do in this situation? I don't usually interact with them for this long. And normally, they're either terrified and lost or grateful that I rescued their child. Well, I suppose now is as good a time as any to practice. "Any chance I can buy your forgiveness with gold? I hear humans really like that stuff."

She blinks and uncrosses her arms, the smile growing more genuine. "Honestly, you can buy my love with gold."

"That's fantastic news. I'm probably going to need it. Hold out your hands." I open my palm above hers and let the coins and dust fall out into her outstretched hand, most of it dropping onto the floor.

"Holy shit!"

"Seriously, Roze?" The bathroom door opens, and Dovana stares at me, hands on her hips, and a playful smirk on her redder-than-usual lips. She's wearing a dark blue dress with a neck that scoops down low enough to remind me that perhaps humans—and this one in particular—are incredibly attractive, and I might not be going along with this because it's predetermined. I can feel my cheeks heating as I try to avert my gaze. "I can't even take five minutes to get ready without you trying to bribe my friends?"

I shrug. "Sorry?"

She rolls her eyes. "It's fine. You're ridiculous."

"You've been in there for almost an hour," Caroline says. "Not five minutes. And I have to pee."

"I'm not used to being around people, and it's basically the only thing I know they like." How on earth am I going to date Dovana when I don't even know how to be around humans? She's a human.

"In all fairness, we really like it," Caroline says in my defense.

Dovana chuckles, looking me up and down with an appreciative grin. I think she likes the dress I made. I didn't even think of trying to make it sexy, just soft. Wow, I very obviously have never dated before. "Well, I hope you don't expect to get by only talking about gold our entire date. And you can't buy me off. You've already given me enough to live off of."

"Of course not. I studied up."

"What, did you read a book on dating? Or maybe you found an interspecies romance book at that place?"

My jaw drops. "Do they have those? That would've been much more helpful."

Her teeth flash in a smile that sends pixies through my belly. "I guess we'll find out when we get there."

"Right." I nod. "Because I could really use that."

"Honestly, I could too."

Caroline looks up at us, her hands full of gold. "Could we maybe not call it interspecies? Just sounds creepy. But you two crazy kids have fun. I'm going to have a nice dinner with Rachel now that I can afford it. Wait, is there a gold exchange place that'd be open now?"

"They close at six," Dovana says. "But you can go tomorrow. I'll take you, and I can give you some cash for dinner in the meantime." She riffles through a bag on the counter and pulls out a leather pouch. "I haven't gone in a bit since we've been busy. Is a hundred okay?"

Caroline grins more broadly than I thought humans could. "That sounds perfect. Thank you."

"Have fun."

"You too. I'll go hang with her after so you can have the room to yourselves."

Dovana's eyes widen. I look between them. What am I missing? "I don't...I mean that's not...okay, fine, thanks, go enjoy your dinner and stop embarrassing me." She pushes a piece of paper into Caroline's hand. "We're going now."

"Wasn't stopping you."

"Did you have a bag or anything?" she asks me.

I shake my head.

"Okay, then, let's go. I'm sure there's a bookshop somewhere in that chaos." She grabs my wrist and tugs me out the door. I follow, still trying to sort out what they were talking about. Do people not normally like having company after a date?

❖

"They really do have a bookshop." Dovana skims over the selection. I've only broken into a few bookshops before, but it seems to be a very small one, taking up only a couple tables near the back of the building, but the subjects are an interesting variety. There are a few romances, some mystery novels, some self-help books—most seeming to deal with addiction and body image—and a few fantasy stories. I assume those are to be read ironically? Like, we'll look at them and be, "Ha, what an absurd idea of what we're like!"

A kindly looking old woman with a few more tentacles and heads than I would expect looks up at me. "If there's something you'd like, I can order it. I only keep a few of the more popular items on hand."

"Oh, that makes sense," Dovana says. "You're like Amazon for fiends?"

"No, that would just be Amazon. I'm Amazon for fiends who don't have addresses or know how computers work."

She chuckles.

"Like the rain forest?" I ask.

"Speaking of fiends who don't have addresses or know how computers work," Dovana says.

"But I've been there."

Dovana smiles at me. "I know you have, Roze, but it's not the same thing. I promise I'll explain it all later or maybe when we're getting dinner if you really want to know."

"Okay…" But I have been there. What don't I understand? She could just explain it now. But I suppose I can wait.

"Were you looking for anything in particular?" the shopkeeper asks.

I shake my head.

"Do you have any books on fiend and human romance?" Dovana asks.

"Just for hypothetical reasons," I insist. We don't know how they might react. That could be violating some rule here.

"Aw, you two are a cute couple. It's rare that a fiend is brave enough to bring their mate around here." She reaches out a tentacle, lightly brushing Dovana's cheek. "Especially such a yummy looking one. I don't think we have any books like that, unfortunately. That bunyip in the diet group tried recently. Though last I heard, she ate him, so maybe not the best source for advice, but if you're desperate, I'm sure Nora could help. You don't eat humans, do you?"

"I do not," I say. I've known a few other monsters who have, but it always seemed rather off-putting.

Dovana cocks her head, studying the woman and pulling away from her appendage. "What diet group?"

"Oh, you don't know? Well, they meet on Wednesdays, so you might have to wait awhile. I'm sure you'll do fine. It's a new millennium, free love and all that."

We both stare at her.

"Oh, in Circe's rotten name, just go enjoy yourselves and stop worrying. And I was only, what, fifty years off? Give me a break. The years all blend together. Darn whippersnappers," she adds with a jovial look.

"No, it wasn't that," Dovana says.

She waves a few tentacles. "Just go have your date. I'll ask around, and next time I see you, I'll let you know if I find anything. Sound fair?"

"Yes, thank you," I say. Wow, I can't believe I'm so committed to this that I'm actually seeking out advice. What would my mother think? Oh, right, she's weirdly okay with this. That's still going to take some getting used to. I was always certain that she wouldn't approve.

"Anytime." She waves again, shooing us off.

"Right, fine, not trying to scare away your ample customers." Dovana looks around the empty stall, the only place that doesn't seem to be completely full of people, emphasizing her point.

Several of her eyes roll.

As we move along in search of a place where we can eat, I say, "I'm glad to see you're making friends already."

"I'm extremely likable, don't you know?"

"Well, you did manage to convince a terrified little girl not to be afraid of humans."

"I did, didn't I?" She beams at me, gazing into my eye, leaning in, and—wait, is she going to—she pulls back and leans against my shoulder. I'm disappointed. I guess that's good news. I know I keep coming to this conclusion, but it's so nice to know that I want her. And so terrifying.

❖

In a corner of the building, there's a makeshift bar, behind which is a table with several large boxes connected to the wall. I assume they're for cooking. I can clean, but modern cooking is unfortunately not magically woven into my very being.

"I guess this is the place," Dovana says. "I knew there had to be something."

"I could put on glasses, and we could find a real restaurant if you'd prefer. I want this to be perfect."

"Oh?" She turns to me, a wicked grin in her eyes. "Trying to woo me now? Just yesterday, you were very desperate to avoid this."

"And I was wrong, and I apologized."

She sighs. "I know. It still hurt to hear."

"I'm sorry."

"Let's eat." She repairs her smile and spins back around, taking my hand and leading me to the counter. "Hi. Is there a menu or anything?"

A horned figure looks her up and down, tilting its head. I really hope it's not going to try to eat her. I was completely bullshitting when I talked my way out of it last time, and I don't remember what I said. "You just buy what you want from the market, and I cook it up. There's no menu. If I don't know the recipe, then you need to bring it."

She blinks repeatedly and stares as if that doesn't quite make sense. "Oh. Okay. I guess we'll go shop."

It shrugs.

"So, what do you want? And no, just bread is not a meal."

I try not to look too crestfallen. "I'm not convinced that is true."

"Seriously. What do you eat? You can't live off honey wheat."

"That's what it's called! Thank you, I always forget, and it makes it much harder to find."

Dovana rolls her eyes. "You need a main course. Or at least some vegetables, cheese, meat, something."

"I normally eat whatever grows in the forest."

Her jaw drops. "No wonder you love bread so much. Laumes don't even cook?"

"My grandmother cooks. She mostly makes stew and the like, but she's sort of weird. I did grow up eating a lot, given how much time I spent with her. She's the only other one who has my gifts as strongly."

She nods. "Right, you've mentioned that before. Well then, let's figure out some food. Any restrictions?"

I start to shake my head but catch myself. "I don't eat meat. I'm not sure if I even can."

"Oh. No wonder you were insistent that laumes don't eat people when we first met."

"We don't." Why does she keep asking this? What in Vaiva's name do people say about us?

"I know." Her hand rests on my shoulder for a moment as she meets my eye. She does understand. She wasn't being the bigoted human my grandmother had filled me with stories about when I was a child. "How about a sandwich?"

"A what?"

Her lips slowly curl up before she finally breaks into a throaty laugh and tears away from me, doubling over. It takes a few long moments for her to collect herself. "I'm sorry. It's kind of hilarious to think that my little bread addict has never had a sandwich."

"What's a sand witch?" I really thought I understood humans better than this. And how many types of witches are there? She could just explain instead of laughing, even if she does have a really cute laugh.

"No, Roze. It's slices of bread with fillings in between. Something like jam or slices of turkey, maybe lettuce and tomato for you?"

I gape at her. "You're pulling my leg."

She shakes her head.

"There are other foods using bread? I mean, I tried that gira, and I've tried kepta duona a few times now, but there are actual whole meals using bread? And you said I couldn't just eat that."

Another laugh. "Well, then, let's go find some honey wheat and something to put on it."

❖

My two toasted honey wheat sandwiches, one with peanut butter and jelly, the other with tomato and lettuce sit on the counter in front of me, taunting me as I wait for Dovana's food to finish cooking. I want to try it so badly, but I've heard that it's rude to start eating before your date, and I'm trying to make a good impression for once.

Finally, her sausage on bread is done and her potato slices covered in cheese and some sort of sauce. I really need to learn what human food is called. The creature sets them in front of her and holds out its hand. "That'll be eight dollars."

"Oh, wow, that's nowhere near as exorbitant as I was expecting," she says, reaching into her bag.

I wave her off. "I've got it." I hold my hand over his and let the gold spill out. "Keep the change." I read that in a dating book.

It stares at the gold before glancing at me and shrugging. "Thanks."

I grin, turning to Dovana, and somehow manage not to ask, 'So we can eat now?' "You were going to tell me about Amazon?"

She giggles, grabbing a piece of potato. "Oh, and help yourself. I got vegan gravy so you could try poutine. I mean, come on, you've been visiting Toronto for over a decade, and I bet you've still never had it."

"I have not."

"Then you better fix that."

But sandwich! I stare at it longingly as I grab a potato sliver and pop it into my mouth. "Hm. That's actually quite good." But bread is better.

"Yay!" She grins so adorably at me that the sandwiches can wait. She changed what she got so she could share it with me. That's very kind of her. Laumes typically tend to ourselves, and I'm not sure it would have ever occurred to me. I'll need to be better than that. "Okay, Amazon is an online thing—"

"Online?"

"Right, I need to explain the internet to you." She takes in a deep breath. "This is going to be very complicated. Basically, a bunch of devices called computers are all hooked up over…um…" She chews on her lip, her eyes unfocused. "It's a magic black market."

"Oh."

"You can buy things and talk to people, all without leaving your home."

"Wow. I had no idea humans were capable of such sorcery."

She pops more poutine into her mouth and grins. "We're pretty impressive. It's not actually magic, though. It's technology. I just don't know how to explain it."

"What's the difference?"

She stares before eating another piece. "I'm a philosophy major. This should be an easier question. I guess the difference is in how understandable it is, but that's not a useful answer when I don't understand it and when sorcerers would understand what they were doing. I'm going to have to think on this for a while."

"Oh, speaking of philosophy, I finished that book you suggested."

"Which one?"

"The Kierkegaard one." I snatch up one of the sandwiches and finally take a bite. By Vaiva. Warm bread. And the ingredients almost melt into it. I could've been putting other food on bread this whole time, and no one told me.

Her face lights up in a massive smile, the light speck of gravy on her lips barely noticeable. "You did? That's amazing. How did you like it? I know he's probably a little too Christian for you, but I really like how he sees the world and contextualizes everything. If you really like him but don't want the religious stuff, I could offer others. I didn't really think about it when I was first talking about him to you, but I had to talk to the class about part of his more religious writings, and it made me think how insensitive I must've been to recommend him to you like that."

"It was fine. I really enjoyed it, and it was nice learning more about how you think."

She cups my cheek. Is she…her thumb brushes against my lips. "You had mayo on you."

I blink. "Oh. There's, um, I think you said it was gravy, on you…should I?"

"Yes. It's fine. Maybe it'd be a bit much for a first date if we hadn't already known each other for years. Unless…" She pulls her hand away and stares at her food. "Did it bother you?"

"No, of course not." I wipe the food from her. "See? I'm fine with it. I just don't know the rules. At all. I didn't even think I'd ever date anyone. Well, I guess that's not true. I knew I would, but I was trying to avoid…you know what, I'm just going to eat this sandwich and let you talk before I manage to break that future now that I'm actually trying for it."

Her laugh doesn't sound too mocking. More friendly. And happy. Genuinely, truly happy, and it's so nice that I would willingly continue to make a fool of myself to hear more of it. She has some of her sausage, blinks and studies it, and then has some more. "Wow, the food here is really good. It tastes so incredibly fresh. Oh. Okay, I guess that makes sense."

I interrupt my filling my mouth with bready goodness. "What?"

"Of course it's fresh. We probably bought it from the very mon…fiend—I don't know if it's a slur exactly, but I'm not taking the risk—who killed it in the first place. No wonder it tastes good."

"I wouldn't know."

"Right. Sorry."

"No, it's fine. I wasn't trying to sound disapproving. I don't mind you eating it. I just don't."

"Okay. Just didn't want to be rubbing it in."

I cock my head. What does that mean? Is it a sex thing? I haven't even thought of that. But it does make sense. That is how tonight ends. But I thought she wanted that. I don't know if I'm really ready for it, but she seemed to be earlier. "You don't want to? I mean, I don't know how else two women—"

Her face turns bright red. "It's an idiom. Sometimes, I forget that you don't know that many English expressions. How did you even learn English anyway?"

"I read books and wrote letters to you."

"That should still teach expressions."

I shrug. "Maybe they didn't make enough sense to me for them to sink in?"

"I guess that makes sense," she says, switching to Lithuanian. "But we don't need to talk in English. It's kinda automatic at this point."

"Thank you. I'm still working on it."

"And you're fantastic. Well past fluent. I just know it can be hard when you don't practice as much. I'm honestly amazed at how good you are at it."

I break into a smile, setting my sandwich down. "Thank you. That means a lot."

"So…" She trails off and gives me a lascivious look. "I believe you were saying something about rubbing?"

"It was a misunderstanding." I stare at her, terrified. I was just thinking how not ready I am for this. What did I set myself up for?

"Yeah, but it shows where your mind is."

"I'm not." Am I? I don't think… "I wasn't. Probably."

"Oh? Probably? And why's that?"

I groan. "Okay, it was a little on my mind, but only because I know how tonight ends."

The smile vanishes from her face, and she stares back at her food but doesn't pick it up. "We don't have to if you don't want to. I know how scared you are about having to follow some predetermined fate."

I nod. "Thank you. I am. I just also, I mean, do you want to?"

"Can I finish my poutine first?"

"I would assume so? You weren't asking to do anything right here, were you?" Well, at least I was right about her wanting it. That makes me feel a little better. Even if it's still terrifying. At least my visions told me that it will be fun. And Zuzane told me that too. That makes it a little less scary.

She chuckles, and it's again worth it. "Good God, Roze, you're hopeless. No, we're not having sex in the middle of a fiend black market. But you look so hot, and I really enjoy spending time with you, and if you want to, I would be okay with it."

"What if I told you that I don't know what it would do to you? The future gets a lot vaguer after the specifics of us getting together. There's the wedding and a few other scant pieces, but fate is harder to read for laumes, and now I'm attached, and I don't know if it might have changed you to affect it too. Since we apparently do this, I don't know if that's why it becomes harder to see our future. Everything would still be in flux, and it's all left very unclear. I don't want to take your humanity away."

Dovana stares at me. "What do you mean?"

"I don't know. No laume has ever been with a human, at least not that I've heard about. I'm not certain exactly what will happen, but the way everything is so precise up until tonight and then is only snippets, well, it has me worried. I know that it's not how changelings work in the west, but what if I turn you into a creature like that?"

She chuckles. "Is this what you've been worried about all these years?"

I shake my head, a bit too quickly judging by the hint of hurt in her eyes. "I've only been thinking about it since last night. I'm not certain of it, but it makes sense. And you do look just a little different at our wedding. Not totally different but slightly changed."

"Well, it is my wedding day. I'm sure there's a bit of a glow."

"Maybe."

"How many eyes do I have?"

"Two."

She squeezes my hand. "Then it's fine. Either it doesn't change me, or it changes me so little that even a laume looking right at me can't tell. Wait, will I be able to make gold?"

I stare at her, trying to see anything clearer in the future, but there's nothing clear beyond the usual glimpses of tonight and the wedding, with bits and pieces too scattered to make any sense of. "I don't know."

She shrugs. "Okay, then. Let's go find out. I've never had risky sex before. Wait, you can't get me pregnant, can you? I don't know how laumes work."

"I cannot."

"Then cool."

"Vaiva, that would make things so much easier. Do you know how much less scared I would've been about us then?"

She smirks. "Well, if you're potentially making a new laume, then it still counts."

"I'm not...you wouldn't be...either way, it wouldn't help the population if you're simply joining the same generation as me."

"I guess that makes sense." She sighs and takes a bite of her food. "Finish your sandwich."

"Okay." We're dropping the subject? I don't know how I feel about that.

"Then maybe we can find out what happens."

I choke on my sandwich. "Oh, so you still...are you sure?"

"Like I said, if you want to. Besides, it's been a while, and I could use it. And it might finally help you relax."

"With how scared I am, I really doubt that," I say.

"Then we won't do it."

I take her hand and meet her eyes. "I'm not here because it's destiny but because there's a reason it's destiny. I enjoy spending time with you, I care for you, and I even love you, if not in the same way as I someday will. I want this." I take a deep breath and close my eye. I know I want this. I can feel it. I can feel a warmth creeping through me just being around her. But I know what it means. There's no turning back if we go through with it. Then again, I'm already here, falling for her. It may already be too late to turn back. And I don't think I'd want to if I could.

She leans in. "Then I do too." Our lips meet, and the honey wheat in my hand is a very distant second place. I fall into it, kissing her back, squeaking in surprise when her tongue slips into my mouth, but I join in and do my best to follow her lead and let it happen. Before I know it, we're back in her dorm room. I don't think we even walked. This is just where I need to be. And I'm so glad of it.

❖

I wake up in her arms to a loud blaring sound coming from the other side of the room. "Sorry," a voice I can't quite place shouts as something slaps against something else, followed by a cluttering sound. Several long moments later, the sound finally stops. "Sorry," she repeats, and I place the voice as Caroline's. Right, this is her room too. When did she finally come home? Should I be embarrassed about being naked? I'm under a blanket, but I don't know the human rules around this. Zuzane always made it sound like humans considered nudity to be a rather unusual thing.

"It's okay," I say.

"No," Dovana says, sounding petulant. "It is not at all okay, and I hate your stupid alarm."

"I'm sorry," she says for the third time.

"I know, and I forgive you, but I still hate it. It's not like there's some better option. Just so long as you don't snooze it, I'm not mad at you."

"Well, I didn't," she shouts cheerily. "It looks like you two had some fun. I had to put the sheet over you."

"Oh. Wow." Dovana grins sheepishly, sitting up and holding the sheet to her chest. I find myself unable to look away. I've never had such bawdy desires. There's not even anything sexual about her chest. Why do I want to see it so badly? "That's embarrassing. Sorry you had to see that."

"It's fine. I'm gonna go shower. If you're going for some wake-up sex, try to be quick about it."

"Of course." Dovana turns her now decidedly less sheepish grin to me. "Is that something we were going to do?"

"I...I...You know, no one else gets me this tongue-tied."

"It seemed to be working fine last night."

I huff. "This is exactly what I mean." I feel a normally welcome sensation. The call. I've never wanted to refuse it before. "But I think I have to..." It grows stronger. Someone must be in serious danger. "Oh, wow, I really have to."

"What? The bathroom?"

"No, I don't do that."

"Wow, then I really hope you turned me into a changeling. That sounds convenient."

I wince. "It's never felt this strong, not even when you were in danger. What's happening?" I try to climb out of bed, and the second my foot steps on the floor, the floor disappears. "Dovana?" I ask, glancing around only to find her absent. Or rather, to find myself absent. I'm not in her room. I'm in a dark cave with lights from a fire flickering from farther along. I try to move away, but I still can't travel in caves. Then how did I get here? That's not how it works.

"Vaiva damn it, Roze," a familiar voice says. "I thought I'd managed to stop you. What a fool I've been. I should've known better."

No. It can't be. Why would she do this? "Grandmother?"

CHAPTER TWENTY-FIVE

DOVANA

What the fuck? She was right here. I mean, I know she can travel like that, but that didn't look like it. Right? She always made it sound so magical. And like she had to move for it, like a Zelazny character walking through worlds. But this time, she just set her foot on the floor and disappeared. And she wasn't even in the woods.

Caroline stares at me, her hand still on the bathroom door. Or rather, she's staring at the spot right in front of me. The spot where Roze just was. "What happened?"

I shake my head. I was still shaking off my dreams a second ago, and now I have this to make sense of. "I don't know. She sounded panicked, right? Like, that wasn't normal?"

She shrugs, staring at me with a look of utter disbelief. "How am I supposed to know? I mean, yeah, it seemed like something was going on, but I don't know. Did you two get up to something weird last night?"

I tilt my head to the side, chewing my lip. "I mean, what's weird?" She was on a date with me. She slept with me. She had a sandwich. That all seems pretty unusual for her. I feel a knot in my stomach along with a pang in my head. What if that wasn't just her normal traveling, and instead it's something to do with our having sex? With her changing me?

"Something she's never done before? Like, it seemed like something was wrong with her."

"Just the one thing," I say looking pointedly down at my bed and the blanket covering my still naked body, trying to emphasize it enough that she won't ask for more details.

"Oh. Wow. You popped a fair...one's cherry." She just barely catches herself.

"Yep."

She leans against the door frame, tapping on the knob and staring at the ceiling. "Does that make them sick?"

"I wouldn't think so? That wasn't one of her concerns."

"Then what were her concerns? Could it be something to do with them?"

"Well, how many eyes do I have?"

"I'm not wearing my glasses."

I stare at her. "Fuck, how blind are you? You can't tell how many eyes I have from seven feet away?"

"Believe it or not, making fun of me does not actually help the situation."

"Sorry," I mutter.

"Wait, did she think she was going to turn you into a laume?"

I shrug. "Kind of?"

"What?"

Waving my hand dismissively, then realizing she may not be able to see that, I say, "Well, it was a fear she had. She didn't really have any evidence or anything. As far as she knows, no laume has ever been with a human, so she wasn't really sure what it might do."

"And could it cause her to teleport away the morning after?"

"I wouldn't think so." I hope. It's only been a few minutes. She's just traveling. I can't start blaming myself yet. "But I don't know."

"There's no way this was intentional, right? Like she's not using you for a one-night stand?"

Would she? She's known me for years. She tried to call off our entire friendship the other day. But then she showed up at my house later without any prompting from me. But I'm the one who kissed her. "It's not impossible, but I've known her for my entire life, and it doesn't at all seem like her. It would be the longest and least efficient way to get a one-night stand I can possibly imagine. Oh God, what if I'm just that bad in bed?"

"Do you need to call Taya and ask?"

"Maybe!" I huff, clutching the sheet tighter. "No. It's not that. Besides, it was her first time. I'm not that experienced, but I know what I'm doing, and I walked her through everything. It wasn't because I was terrible or anything. And that wouldn't explain how she acted this morning. Or why she went back for seconds. Or thirds."

"Didn't need quite that many details."

"You absolutely did."

She crosses her arms, glaring in my general direction. "Okay, what do you know? How does her teleporting work?"

"I thought she could only do forest to forest, but she mentioned recently that she can do houses too. It just doesn't come as naturally to her. And last night when we kissed, she managed to teleport us out of that Quaker place to here without even taking a step. But she wasn't sure how she did it either, so I'm not sure if that's how she did this."

"Maybe falling in love gives laumes extra powers?"

My cheeks feel like they're on fire. "We're not. She's not. I'm not. Wait, that, I…"

"You can process your emotions after we find out if your girlfriend is in danger."

"I don't think she's my girlfriend."

"Really? What happened to lesbian speed? I know you've told me that you're supposed to be girlfriends by the end of the first date."

I grumble. "I didn't say quite that. I don't think that's a thing… The getting powers, I mean. We absolutely fall in love fast and hard. And better."

"I don't know about better."

"No, definitely better."

She groans. "Fine, whatever, now that you're in love, and I'm not—"

"I'm not in love!" Probably. Like, I don't think I can say I'm "in love," but I do love her. I sigh. "At least, not yet. It's new. But I need to see if this is really my destiny. If this is really what I want. I can't lose her now."

"You do think something's wrong, then?"

I nod. "It has to be. She wouldn't simply vanish. I mean, maybe she would, but I don't think she did." Her eager smile looking up at me is burnt into my brain. Her lips still glistening with... Well, heartache, worry, and horniness are a terrible combination, so I try not to focus on that. "She wouldn't. She'd maybe go to rescue someone, but she'd be back, and she would've said something less cryptic." Had that been what she was referring to? She did say she had to do something. But why wouldn't she be back? And how would she travel inside my dorm room?

She sighs. "Okay. I can skip class. We'll get to the bottom of this."

"No. Thank you, but no. I don't think there's anything you can do. I don't even think there's anything I can do." A twinge of something not quite like pain hits the back of my head, and I wince and have to search my thoughts for what I was saying. "There's nothing I can do. Just go to class. Right. I'm going to go talk to Taya, make sure she's okay, and then maybe I'll try going back to the...shit, it's probably actually a Quaker place right now. Maybe I'll just go to class then."

"Are you sure? I really don't mind."

"I'm sure." I start to stand and am reminded of my nudity, so I wrap the sheet around me before heading over to her. "It's okay." I look into her eyes now that I'm close enough that she can properly see me and rest my hands on her shoulders. "I appreciate it. But teleporting girlfriends don't seem to be a, gather all your girl-friends and cry over some drinks and ice cream, sort of situation. I think something is wrong, but I don't even know what it is yet. It could be that some kid was in serious danger, and she'll be back in a little while, or hell, maybe a house really needed cleaning. Or maybe she had to get whisked away to be knocked up by some centaur or something. I have no idea. I'm scared, but I'm not going to dissolve into tears over something this confusing. Just go to class, and I'll try to figure this out." I've already dragged her into too much. I nearly got her eaten because of how badly I wanted to find Roze. I can stomach putting Taya through that—she earned it after sending me into counseling—but Caroline has done enough.

"But—"

"I promise, if I don't have an answer by the time you're home, then you can help."

"Okay." She sighs, looking like she wants to cry. "I'm just worried about you. She's already put you through so much, and I know this one probably isn't her fault. I'm not saying that. But it doesn't change that it's a lot of stress for you."

"And I'll be okay. Just go shower."

"Fine." She gives me a lopsided grin and finally opens the door. "Let me know the second she gets back so I can stop worrying for you."

"Of course. I'll text you."

"Thank you."

Another twinge at the back of my head, but I shake it off. I said I'd talk to Taya. I should do that. I need to make sure she's not having a jealous breakdown or anything. Maybe she'll have better advice on Roze. Or at least she can assure me that I'm not so terrible in bed that it would make Roze disappear before my eyes.

❖

"Fuck off, Aaron," she yells when I knock on her door. "My music isn't even that loud. I'm sleeping. Go away."

I stare at the door. Metal in a language I can't quite place filters out. She used to use headphones back when she had a roommate. Must be nice. "Sorry, your Soviet anthem was keeping me up in the next building over."

Three seconds later, the door opens, revealing her in a tank top and boy shorts. "Sorry, Vana. I didn't realize it was you."

"I gathered. Neighbors been giving you trouble?"

"Not too much. Just whining a few days a week." She heads back toward her bed, waving for me to follow.

I do so, letting the door close behind me. "You okay?" Gah! My head. It still doesn't exactly hurt, but it keeps getting more intense. What the hell is that? I don't get migraines, and aren't they supposed to be more at the temples? The back of my head just keeps aching. It's like this weird pulling, like a finger hooked inside my head, trying to tug me around. It can't even fairly be described as pain, and yet it feels like my head is going to split open.

"Yeah. Why?" She plops back onto her bed, yawns, blinks repeatedly, and stretches. "Other than some insensitive bitch waking me up, at least."

"Okay, just wanted to make sure."

Her eyes shoot back open. "Wait. Why're you here so early? Did something happen with Roze?"

I screw my eyes shut, trying to ignore the weird headache thing. "Well, I was gonna say it was fantastic, but something weird happened this morning."

She throws herself to her feet, looking right into my eyes. "What did she do? I'll fucking kill her."

"Oh my God, Taya, no. Nothing like that. She, kind of... disappeared."

"So she vanished without even leaving a note? Of course. I should've known."

"No. She literally disappeared. We woke up together to Caroline's alarm, and then she said something was happening, and she disappeared."

"So she—"

"No. It wasn't some weird one-night stand thing. I already went over all of this with Caroline. This was weirder. This was magical stuff, and I'm worried about her, but I don't know what to do. I didn't want to worry Caroline, but the more I think about...aahh" That finger just keeps curling. And not in a fun way. This must be how Zeus felt when Athena popped out of his head.

She gulps and reaches out for me, but hesitates. "What?"

I shake my head. "Nothing. I've been getting these headaches all morning. I don't know what's up with them."

"That's new."

"Ya think? Sorry. It is. It doesn't even really hurt. It's more like this weird intense thudding demanding my attention."

"Want some Motrin?"

I wave her off. "I think I'm okay. It's dying back down. What was I saying?"

"Something was wrong, and you didn't want to worry your roommate, so you came to the one person you knew could actually help?"

"Right, because you have magic powers."

"I've been told so by quite a few women."

I glare at her. "I'm not saying you're bad by any means, but I think that's taking it a bit far."

"Okay, fine." Aw, she actually looks kinda hurt. "You were saying?"

"Sorry. You were fantastic."

"Damn right I was." She grins.

I chuckle. "She started talking about this weird intense call. She was even wincing from it. She's talked about it in her letters before, but it never sounded painful. It was this call that she'd feel that just seemed urgent, willing her to it. And she'd take a few steps and be there. And the sensation…" It thuds in the back of my head. "It would keep gnawing at her until she went to it. At least, I think that's how she described it. It always seemed really abstract. But this morning was different."

"Vana?" She's staring, her hands are on my shoulders, and she looks concerned. Was I doing something?

"I'm fine." I shake her off. "But it shouldn't be able to…fuck." I have to take a few deep breaths in order to make myself focus. It won't stop. It's like this insistent thudding in the back of my head demanding my attention. Something calling at me. Almost like… wait, calling? "Fuck."

"What?"

I blink. I guess it was because of the sex. "Well. That might answer that." Could it really have turned me that quickly? Am I really being called? Can I just go walk in the woods and find out where I'm supposed to be? How does it even work?

Her eyes widen. "Dovana, what? You're really starting to scare me."

"I think I'm a changeling."

CHAPTER TWENTY-SIX

ROZE

Grandmother?" I repeat, walking down the long passageway of her cave. I haven't been this far in since I was a child. Assorted magical items line the walls. Some of them are in jars, likely stolen or traded for from humans, but most are out on their own or in bags that she must've weaved herself. I don't recognize all of the herbs and body parts, though I've seen her use many of them before. That tail, the mushroom, and that flower can be brewed along with the stomach of a deer to create a tincture that will cure the flu. She's saved a few villages with that in her day. "Are you here, Grandmother?" I ask again. Surely, she must be around here somewhere. I heard her voice a few minutes ago. Oh no.

I pick up the pace, not taking time to inspect her stores. What if that's why the call felt urgent. I've never had a family member die. Could that be what this is? Is that how I got here? I run as fast as I can, my bare feet beating against the damp floor. "Grandmother?"

When I find her, she doesn't look ill or dying. She's simply sitting at the same table I dined with her at earlier this week, drinking some tea. "Roze," she says, and her voice lacks any of its usual warmth.

"What is it, Grandmother? Do you know why I'm here? I felt the call stronger than I ever have, and before I knew it, I was in your cave. I didn't think I could do that."

She shakes her head, looking on me with sad eyes as she gives a weary sigh. "I spent so long teaching you right from wrong, dear child. How could you do this?"

"What? I didn't do anything."

"Even still, you lie to me."

I stare at her, unable to process what she's saying. Why is she acting like this? I don't think I've ever....well, I guess I kind of lied about Dovana, but it wasn't anything major. I told her what was going on. I just didn't give her all of the details. That's hardly a lie. "I don't understand."

"Then you're a bigger fool than I took you for. Mere hours ago, you forsook your family, doomed your kind to extinction, and corrupted a poor thing you were meant to save. I tried to stop it, to bring you here, but in your madness, your mind was too far gone for even my gifts to reach."

"What?" The room blurs, and I have to blink away tears. Why is she talking like this? This isn't my grandmother. She was always understanding and supportive. She taught me so much about the world.

She swings her hand, sending the teacup hurling across the cave to clatter against the wall and fall to the floor. "Stop playing naive!"

I take a deep breath and swallow a lump in my throat. "Our kind is dying no matter what, Grandmother."

"There is still hope. There is always hope. And yet instead of doing your duty as your mother's daughter, you bewitched a creature in your care."

"I did nothing of the sort." I let out a shuddering breath, tears clouding my vision. "I have spent years fearing that. Knowing that I was going to betray what you taught me and trying to find a way not to. But we have to accept that we're dying out." If I don't tell myself that, I don't know if I can live with it.

She climbs out of her chair, glowering up at me as her cloven hooves stomp on the dirt. "The girl, Dovana. Do you really think I do not know what you did to her? She was a human, meant to be cared for and saved while we live our separate lives. I tried to teach you not to interfere with her fate, and yet you saw fit to ignore every word of wisdom I ever gave you."

"I did no such thing." I feel like such a child, petulantly refusing everything she says. Well, no more. I have to stand up for myself. I've decided to embrace my destiny. It terrifies me. I feel sick just admitting it to myself. But the only thing that's ever felt as right as fulfilling my calling is being with her. "I did exactly as you bid me. I spent my entire life ignoring her fate, but you said to allow it to happen, so I did precisely as I saw. I comforted her after I'd hurt her, I went out with her, and I loved her. And I know that I'm going to continue loving her in every meaning of the word, just as her fate has said since we first met. I didn't betray my kind. I fulfilled my very purpose."

"You lie!" She stomps her hoof again.

I step forward, towering over her. "I do not."

"No laume would ever be destined to be with a human, if you can even call her that anymore. It's not how we're meant to be."

I grit my teeth, clenching my fist at my side. She can hate me for this, but Dovana doesn't deserve that. "But it is how I am meant to be, Grandmother. I tried very hard to ignore what you said, but you were right. Sometimes, you can't change fate. And I was a fool to want to." Thinking of last night, I can't help but smile, even when staring at the very woman who convinced me to dread it in the first place. "You always told me how important it was for us to carry on the line, to find someone and breed. You taught me how important it was to my mother. She'd said it too, of course, but it was you, you were the one who made me question my destiny. Weren't you?"

"I would never," she stammers, taking a step back. "It simply cannot be your fate. I would have known it, and I'd have stopped it."

"You really didn't know?"

"Of course not. I...I would have not allowed your mother to take you out to rescue people."

I sigh. "Perhaps that's the only way this could have been averted, but you know how much a part of me that is. I could never have resisted the call. You'd have had to tie me up in the back of your cave and never let me out."

"Then perhaps I'll do exactly that."

"You will not. Grandmother, it's too late. Not even you can change this fate. I certainly couldn't."

"But—"

I kneel, meeting her gaze and resting my hand on her shoulder. "It is done, Grandmother. There's no point in trying to change it now."

Tears form in her eye. I'd expected more anger or defiance, hell, even understanding, but not this. "You have brought shame upon this family and doomed us all. And more than that, you have turned the very first girl in your care into a vile being that should not be."

"What are you talking about? You keep saying things like that, but I thought you were being metaphorical. What did I do to Dovana? Wait, was I right? I was sure I was being crazy, looking for another excuse. No one had ever told me anything like that. I thought maybe it would have some weird effect." I don't know how I feel. I want to feel guilty for corrupting the woman I...the woman I'm to wed. But at the same time, it's nice to know that I'm not alone. That I can spend my life with not only my best friend but another laume.

"Some weird effect," she spits, mocking the words. "You have turned her into a creature not fit for either world. I hadn't even truly believed it possible. And I certainly didn't think any laume would be fool enough to try it."

"If she's unfit for our world, then it's because of those like you. If you're right, and I've changed her, then it's all the more reason we should welcome her as one of us. But all you give me is poetic waxing without any actual claim. Honestly, it's like trying to parse that Kierkegaard book but more insulting. There's nothing wrong with her. I saw her this morning. Maybe this is another fear you implanted in me."

She shakes her head, and something in her eye gives me pause. "I don't know what will happen, dear child. But you have done something to the girl, something that cannot be undone."

I want to argue, to fight back against the claim; it's the first argument I've ever had with her, and I was hoping to let the anger carry me for a little while, but it's hard when she sounds more concerned than anything. "What is it?"

"I can't know without seeing her. I looked into your life, into you, and I saw her being unmade."

My cheeks heat. "You watched that?"

She waves her hand. "Don't be so human. Next, you'll be ashamed of your nudity. I'm not sure that I'll ever be able to forgive you for what you've done, but if this is indeed your destiny, then allow me to learn what I can. Your visions never shared anything of her fate?"

I shake my head. "No. It all went rather vague after we got together. I mostly saw our wedding."

"Please say it wasn't a human affair."

My shoulders droop. Great, where's that fight in me when I need it? "It will be."

She groans. "Who am I to argue with the future?" She takes another look at me without any particular emotion. Is she trying to see my fate? If it was that easy for her, you'd think she'd have done it before. "Though it seems she'll be here on her own by tomorrow if we wait. Perhaps that is a destiny we can change."

She's still so fixed on stopping me from being with her. Even now that it's already too late. Now that I actually want it.

CHAPTER TWENTY-SEVEN

DOVANA

W hat do you mean you're a changeling?" Taya asks. "Like, the sort that replace human babies but are actually centuries old?"

"No, not like that. I mean, I assume not like that. It's at least not what she was saying. She didn't replace me with a fair one." I would know that, right? Yeah, changelings always know; they're just hiding from everyone around them. Kinda like Roze was.

She stares.

"She'd been worried about this. She thought that us...well... doing that could have some effect on me."

"I'm a big girl, Vana. You don't need to sugarcoat it."

I roll my eyes. "She didn't seem terribly sure of what she meant, and I dismissed it as another fear and reason not to see each other. But I think that's what this feeling is. It sounds like the call that she always describes. There's this intense prickling in the back of my head, demanding my attention, but I don't quite know what it is. I think she might be in danger."

"I'm sorry, you're skipping like a million steps. You think you're a fairy because you have a headache?"

"No! I mean, yes. But stop saying that word. I'm not even sure if I would actually count as a fair one. I mean, I guess I would, but I'm still human. I think. I am human, aren't I?"

She takes my hand. Confusion is still abundantly clear on her face, but concern seems to be overwhelming it. "Of course you're human. You're my Dovana. That annoying girl I got stuck with in my freshman dorm. You're you. No matter what you've done or what happens, that won't change. I still kind of think you're talking crazy, but I've learned by now that I should just believe what you say. So if you're a changeling, then, okay. You're a changeling. But you're still human too. Isn't that what would make you a changeling? You'd be of both worlds. Part human and part fae."

I nod, swallowing the lump in my throat. "Yeah. I guess that's true. It's all a little over...gah." It's getting stronger. "That fucking thing eating away at the back of my head. It's like there's something wrong with Roze, and she needs me. I have to go to her. She's scared. I can feel it."

"How will you find her? It took luck and almost getting killed the first time."

I turn, releasing her hand and the comfort it gives me. I have to do this. If I don't...Roze was never too specific about it, but it sounded like there wasn't much of a choice in ignoring these calls. "I can find her. I can feel her." I start taking a few steps, as if I'm trying to triangulate her or maybe teleport. If I had any idea how to do that, it would be a lot easier. That finger keeps pulling at my head, but it doesn't even suggest what to do. I'm just wandering around trying to see if it changes. I really wish I had more of a plan. "It feels almost familiar. Not just because it's her, but because it's... maybe she's back home?"

"You think she's back in your village?"

I shake my head. "No. But Lithuania, definitely. If I was just there, then I'd be able to find her. I could get in a car and drive until I was there. The country isn't that big. It wouldn't take more than a few hours."

"Okay. Sure. Let's go to Lithuania. Sounds fun."

I turn back around, staring. "What? No. You have class."

"So do you. I'm coming with."

"I need to do this alone."

She takes a step, those warm brown eyes staring into me. "No. You're transforming into something, and you have this feeling that's so intense it's cutting you off mid-sentence. I'm not letting you do this alone. You'd crash. You need help."

"But—"

"No arguing. If you're going, I'm going with you."

"Oh, fine. It's not like arguing with you has ever helped." I try to glare at her, but I can feel my smile. As much of a bitch as she is, she really is my best friend.

"You're one to talk."

"You want to call a cab?"

She snorts. "You're the one with the unlimited gold. Why would I call? Hell, can you make it yourself now?"

I hold out my hand, spread out my fingers, and try to will coins to fall to the floor. Nothing happens. "No idea. I didn't exactly get an instruction manual."

"Well, then, I'm glad you have a bank account."

It's not like it's lacking. Being given a fortune every year really adds up. "Okay, sure." I pull my phone out of my purse and order a cab to the airport. "It should be here in fifteen minutes."

"Great. I've always wanted to go to Lithuania."

"Why? Hoping to shoot up a TV station or something?"

She puts her hands on her hips and glares. "You do realize I'm not a soviet, right? Like, I'd think by now you would know that, but I'm really starting to wonder."

I roll my eyes. "Pretty sure you are."

"Pretty sure I'm not."

I glare back.

"Should I pack clothes?"

Oh. Shit. I hadn't thought of that. "I don't know? I mean, we're only going for the day, right?"

"Yeah, but the flight is like all day already, isn't it?"

"Probably. I haven't bought the tickets yet. Eh, whatever, we can buy some clothes at the airport. Grab your passport. They'll be here in a couple minutes." My mom is going to flip that I just ran back home without a word. Maybe she'll forgive me if I grab her some booze from the duty-free store.

She shrugs. "If you insist. I'm not going to say no to free clothes."

I lead the way and open the door, only to step outside and run into someone. "Oof."

"There you are," a familiar voice says. Roze. But how? We're not in Lithuania yet. Did I teleport?

"What the fuck?" Taya's voice behind me confirms that I am still in Toronto.

"So this is the being you corrupted." I pull away to meet the owner of the new voice. She's an old woman wearing a long gown and a scarf around her head.

I turn back to my…whatever she is. Aw, she put on clothes. "I'm so glad you're okay. Who's this?"

"Grandmother, you said you would stop saying that."

The old woman waves, dismissing the comment. I'm already meeting her family. And she's mean. Maybe I should disappear. Turnabout is fair play. And then I don't have to deal with an ornery babushka. But then Roze still would. And I'd have no idea what was going on. Also, I don't know how to teleport.

"She didn't corrupt me."

She fixes me with a glare that sends a shiver up my spine. "Get back into the room and let me have a look at you."

"But this is my room," Taya mutters.

"We have a taxi," I add.

"I don't know what that is," the old woman says.

I groan. "Oh, fine. I guess we're not going anywhere anyway." I cancel the car and follow the bitchy old babushka into my ex-girlfriend's bedroom. That's not a sentence I ever expected to say.

"Have a seat." She sounds more like a doctor than the witch she looks like.

"What's going on?" Taya asks.

Roze takes my hand, her thumb hesitantly running along my knuckles. "My grandmother is simply concerned. Apparently, what Dovana and I did can have some consequences, but we're not quite sure what they are. She wants to make sure there's nothing to worry about."

I stare at her. "Should I be worried?"

"Of course not."

Taya clears her throat, and we all turn to her. "So she shouldn't be concerned you're bringing some old witch into my apartment after she's already been freaking out? She's had a weird headache since you left, and now you come back like nothing's wrong to do some weird medical checkup, and none of that is something to be concerned about?"

"Taya..." I have no idea what to say. She's not wrong. I'm just not sure what it's going to accomplish. We'll find out if there's anything to worry about after my future grandmother-in-law checks me out. "Wait, Roze, you weren't in danger? It really felt like it."

A soft smile graces her lips as she slips an arm around me. "You can feel it, then? I didn't expect that. And yeah, I suppose I was. She'd kidnapped me, but we sorted it out."

"She what?"

"Turns out that my grandmother was a big part of why I thought humans were awful, and she freaked out a bit when I started dating one."

"It wasn't the dating I was concerned with," the withered old kidnapping bitch says. "The end result of that dating is almost certainly what caused this little issue. Open your mouth."

"I'm sorry?" She sticks her finger in my mouth and pushes against the roof. "The fuck?" I attempt to say, only for it to sound more like "A ug?"

"I thought we'd already had this conversation?"

"Huh?" I manage around her finger.

"I'm always bad about that. I need to examine you, lest your body fall apart without our knowing. Okay?"

Well, when she puts it like that... "Okay."

"I need to learn what this is doing to you." She pulls a bag out of nowhere and sets it on the bed. When she opens it with the hand not in my mouth, the smell coming from it is enough to make me want to vomit on her. She sticks her finger in it, then adds that to the one already in my mouth. I have to swallow my bile. It tastes like rotten death.

She runs her finger along the inside of my mouth and pulls it back out, staring at it. "Hmm."

"Did that tell you anything, or are you just a complete creep as well as a bigoted asshole?"

Her eye narrows, and I find myself sitting up straight with my legs close together. All Lithuanian grandmothers must have the same glare, as I've been fixed with that one too many times. At least they don't look alike. Mine has two eyes. "How do you feel?"

"Like you stuffed moldy dung in my mouth."

"Hmm," she says again. I'm really starting to hate her. "This tastes foul to you?"

"It's like eating powdered asshole."

She turns to Taya. "You, human thing."

"Taya."

She shrugs. "What does this taste like?" She holds the bag out, and Taya gives it a hesitant sniff.

"Do I have to?"

"Yes."

Groaning, she glares at the bitch, dips a finger in, then licks it off. "I dunno, like some weird artificial sweetener? Definitely not as bad as Vana is acting like."

"What? Are you kidding? That's the most horrid thing I've ever tasted."

"It reeks," Roze confirms.

The bitch nods, considering this. "Well, that's not a great sign. I need to run about twenty more tests."

"No," I say firmly.

"I wasn't asking. There's work to do if we want to make sure you don't fall apart."

I blink. "You were being literal about that?"

"I'm not certain precisely what will happen. We're not supposed to produce changelings, so this is uncharted territory. Now let's get this over with. I enjoy this no more than you."

"I doubt that."

"But this is my room," Taya says. "I have class."

"Then go," she replies, waving a withered old hand.

"But it's my room. Oh, and I take it we're not going to Lithuania, Vana?"

I start to say something only for a finger to go back in my mouth, so I shake my head instead.

"Fuck it. Fine. You all have fun. The door locks automatically, just make sure it closes all the way." She grabs her backpack and heads toward the door, then stops and looks at me. "Vana, text me if anything happens. I'll rush back here."

I nod.

"Okay. Don't light anything on fire. I don't want to get kicked out because of some weird magic shit. God, what has my life become? If the old broad gives you too much trouble, you can always bite her fingers off." She slams the door behind her, leaving me to be poked and prodded with only Roze to look after me.

Roze tightens her grip around my shoulders. "It'll be okay. I promise. She's not up to anything duplicitous, and I'd stop her if she tried. I just need to make sure you're all right."

I nod again as another finger presses against my cheek. "Ank oo."

It takes hours. And some fire, which Taya will not be thrilled about, but finally, I receive my diagnosis. "I don't know what will happen from here. It may not progress any further, but it can't be changed back. You've been infected by my fool of a granddaughter."

"She's not a fool."

Roze squeezes me.

"But it's too late to change that. Take good care of her, and if anything more develops, she can get me. Until then, I suppose, welcome to the family." She sounds so thrilled. I feel about the same. I already hate my future grandmother-in-law.

Chapter Twenty-eight

Roze

Dovana sits on her friend's bed with bruises on both shoulders and dried blood on her upper arm. My grandmother was very thorough with her investigation. Taya returned a few minutes ago and is now glaring at us from the desk a few feet away. My grandmother left maybe ten minutes ago. She said that she had to double-check everything, but that Dovana should at least be able to survive in her new state. It's so strange to think that I could've killed her. But then again, I suppose I always knew that it wouldn't. She made it to our wedding and the few glimpses I saw beyond. Does that mean even this entire affair with my grandmother was predestined?

"Are you okay?" Taya asks. "The hell did that bitch do to you?"

She sighs, leaning against my shoulder. "Mostly poked and prodded every orifice and tried to create a few more."

"I'm sure I could find something iron to stab her with."

"Just be careful around me with it," she says, a pained expression on her face but only for a moment. It vanishes, and something between acceptance and contentment replaces it. "I can handle it on my outside, but it really burns on the inside."

"Did she stab you with it or—" She made a circle with one hand and crudely pushed her finger in and out of it.

"Only stabbed," she shouts, bolting back to a sitting position. "Nothing like that. God, get your head out of...just...no."

Taya shrugs. "You're the one that said every orifice."

Dovana rolls her eyes. "Okay, can we please stop going over this? It's been like four hours of being experimented on, and I'd rather not relive it."

"But can you still eat food that has iron in it?"

She blinks, cocks her head, groans, and falls back until her head dangles off the other side of the bed. "Fuck. I don't actually know. Probably not? Like, it gets in your blood. Goddamn it, I am going to have to be extremely careful about food now if I don't want to feel like my skin is on fire for a few days. Hours? How long does it take for iron to pass through?"

"I can look it up if you want."

"No, I'll look into it later."

"There's iron in food?" I ask. How can they do that? Are they trying to poison the fae? Or make sure we don't eat their bread?

"Humans need iron to live," Taya says.

"What?" My jaw drops. "No wonder you're all scary! Of course you go around killing monsters. You fucking eat iron. What else do you eat? Lava?"

"Now that would be spicy."

"We don't eat lava," Dovana says. "Or they don't? This is going to take some getting used to."

I try pulling her to me, but she stays where she is, so I pat her shoulder instead. If she needs time to grow accustomed to this, then she can have it, I know how things will go. And I may need that time as well. I feel the urge to have her in my arms, as strongly as any call, but it still terrifies me. "You're human. But not only human anymore. I'm sorry for that. I really thought I was being crazy. It made sense in my head, but I assumed someone would have told me about it before if it was a real thing."

She shakes her head, her dangling hair swishing against the bed. "No. It's okay. I'm really not upset with you. At least I already know I'm going to be happy like this."

I offer a smile that she can't see. "That *is* nice to know. I focused so much on how scary the idea was that I never really thought about how happy we always looked together."

She reaches up, taking my hand and pulling herself back to a sitting position. "I was already pretty damn happy on that first date. I don't know what the future holds—other than what you've said—but I think we have something good here. And I'm excited to see exactly how it goes, now that I finally have the chance."

"I'm sorry about that."

She chuckles and leans in, kissing my cheek. "It's okay. At least you finally wised up."

"Get a room," Taya says.

"We're in one."

"Yes. Mine."

"Close enough."

Taya taps her fingers on the plastic box on her desk. "I have shit to do. If you two are going to canoodle, can I at least do my homework in peace? Or do you need to keep using my room as an improvised gynecologist's office?"

"I said we're not talking about that," Dovana says firmly.

"Then you two can go have fun and not talk about it."

The two of them exchange silent glances while I'm left holding her hand and wondering what's going on. "All right," Dovana finally says. "I'll stop rubbing it in your face. I love you, Taya. Talk to you tomorrow?"

It takes a moment, but she nods. "Yeah. Of course. Same time, same place. Get going." She jerks her head toward the door. "I really have to work on this paper."

"Okay." She nods and stands, tugging gently on my hand. "Well, you heard her. Let's go have some fun. I bet you've never even seen a movie."

"What's a movie?"

She grins. "That's what I thought. Let's go find out."

❖

I expect her to take me back to that fiend bazaar, but instead, she leads me to her dorm room. I'd been there looking for her a few hours ago. "Movies are here?" I ask, sounding almost as confused as I feel. She still hasn't told me anything.

"Yes," she says, sounding a little condescending. "Movies are, in fact, here." She tugs on my hand. "Come on. I'll show you. You can even pick if you want."

"But what is a movie? What would I be picking?"

She sighs, tapping her foot on the carpeted hallway. "It's really easier to show you. And besides, I know how you are about these hallways, so stop fighting and let's hurry up."

I hesitate but quickly give in. It's not like I'll learn anything standing out here. And she is right about not being comfortable. I'd really rather not end up revealing myself to a whole bunch of humans the second I decide to break from tradition. I suspect my grandmother would have a whole new lecture for me then. "Okay, fine. Let's find out what these movies are. I don't know why you have to be secretive about everything."

"Roze, dearest, I don't think you even know what a TV is."

I stare at her.

"Like I said. It'll take some explaining." She opens the door and ushers me inside where I find Caroline and a girl I don't recognize sitting on the other bed. I turn back around, walking into Dovana, and see the door across the hall open. Can't go that way either.

Dovana catches me by the shoulders as she shoves the door closed with her foot. "Whoa, you okay, Roze?"

"Oh, hello," the new girl says.

"Oh," Dovana says.

"Shit," Caroline mutters. "Um, Rachel." She clears her throat. "We should get out of here."

"What?"

"Erm," she stammers.

"Well," Dovana tries.

I keep staring at the girl I'm dating, not willing to turn around. It's not like revealing myself is some horrid thing. It's just that I've already introduced myself to two new humans this week who weren't in any danger or even in need of housekeeping. Any time humans learn about us, they start doing stupid things to get gold, like sending their children out into the cold night on their own. In addition to the fact that I'd rather a child not suffer, it then means we have to kill the bastard, and I'd be loath to ever do so.

"Who's this?" Apparently-Rachel asks.

"That's Roze," Caroline says dismissively. "She's Dovana's... um, what are you two right now, actually?"

"I don't even fucking know," Dovana mutters. "Hey, Rachel, why don't you two go get dinner? I'll pay, and you can bring us back something?"

"Okay..." She sounds confused, but I don't risk glancing back. "Anything you want in particular?"

"She's a vegetarian but just some sort of pizza. I promise she'll go crazy for that."

Pizza? I know I've seen that mentioned in something before.

"Okay...is everything okay?"

"Why don't you go on to the bathroom?" she whispers, lightly pushing me toward the door to my right. "She just has a really bad bloody nose."

"Oh no. What happened?"

"Um," she stammers. "Allergies?"

"Really?"

I hurry in and close the door behind me. "Yes. Definitely allergies," she says, not at all convincingly. I wish my visions had told me more about this. I've always hidden away from humanity, and it's never bothered me before. But now I'm hiding away from her life. Or *our* life. It hurts.

Footsteps sound under the door. "But she'll be okay?" the girl asks.

"Yeah. It always happens. Don't worry about it."

"Okay. Well, it was nice meeting you, Rose." A door slams, and someone knocks on the door behind me.

Dovana's voice follows. "It's okay. You can come out now. They're gone."

I take a deep breath and peer out, relieved to see the coast is clear. Maybe once Grandmother has calmed down, I could talk to her about a spell to hide my nature or some other options. "This is going to be complicated, isn't it?"

She gives me a crooked smile. "You could always just show yourself and not worry about it. Or wear sunglasses. Maybe even just long bangs. It's not like you have goat legs to hide, no offense to your mother or anything. She's a lovely woman. And she could easily conceal them with some pants."

Chuckling, I lean against the door frame. "So what's pizza? Or do I have to wait and see like the movie?"

"Yep." She grins, looking as mischievous as she does gleeful. If I hadn't already decided to kiss her, then that look would've done it. I lean in. She lets out a surprised squeak but gives in, wrapping her arms around me. When she finally pulls away, the grin looks a tad more lascivious. "You sure you're up for all that?" she asks. "I mean, I know we've done it before, but it's a big change from what you were used to."

"I'm going all in on this. We're going to be together, and so far, I'm quite enjoying it, so I don't see any reason to hold back."

She shrugs. "All right. Though, boy, you do not make it sound romantic."

I nod, feeling tears welling up. "I'm sorry. I'm used to trying with all my might not to let it be romantic." Taking her hand, I say, "I'm not doing this because I know I can. I'm doing this because I want to. I like you, and I always knew I would. I'm just finally seeing how true it can be."

She gulps, her eyes darting to my lips. "Okay, that was a pretty good line. Maybe I can even manage to believe it."

"It's the truth, Vana. Why are you doing this? What makes you want me?"

She blinks and purses her lips. "Can't I just say you look really sexy in those dresses?"

"I suppose you can, but I'd certainly like more of an answer than that. Though, given what all I've put you through this last week, I may deserve waiting for it."

She shakes her head and makes a low groaning sound. "I don't know. I'm sure part of it is that I know it's possible for us to have a really amazing life because you've already seen it, but I don't think that's the main reason." She sighs. "I suppose it's because talking to you has always been the most important part of every year. Just seeing your letter, making or picking your gift, all of it has been important to me for so long. And I don't know if it would've happened if you hadn't said anything, but those feelings grew, and you became important to me yourself. Now, the idea that I can be with you and feel like that every day, well, it's pretty fucking great."

Retreating to the bathroom again almost sounds tempting. It feels like someone put an iron mask on me, my cheeks are burning so hard. "That's a pretty good reason. And way more of one than you'd given before."

"I've had time to think about it."

I smile, her words still flowing through my brain and preventing any possibility of a further reply.

She chuckles. "So want to find out what a movie is?"

"Yes. You keep refusing to tell me. Please. It sounds important. And it's been driving me crazy."

That same mischievous look returns. "Maybe I should make you suffer. I'm sure we could think of something else to do."

"But I want to know," I whine.

"I know you do. But all this romantic talk has other ideas in my head. I'm sure we have at least an hour before they get back." Her hand rests on my lower back, and she closes the distance between us, her eyes staring into mine. "Plus, the pitiful noise you make when you want to know something is very cute."

I grumble.

"How about we head over to my bed, and I keep showing you how badly I really do want this, and then maybe once the pizza gets back, I'll show you what a movie is?" Her yelp of surprise is the only thing that clues me in to our location having changed. I was too busy watching her. "I'll take that as a yes." She giggles, pushing me back on the bed, and trails kisses down my jaw. "By the time

I'm done with you, you won't even remember what question was nagging at you."

❖

The door opens somewhere between a few minutes and a few hours later. "Do you have clothes on?" Caroline calls from the door.

"Nope," Dovana replies, her tone mirthful.

"I talked Rachel into heading home. This better not be a recurring thing. I need to be able to have friends."

"We'll figure it out." She waves dismissively. "Worse comes to worst, she can find out about laumes."

"Yeah, that would go great. Pizza is on the counter. Let me know when you're dressed. I'll be in the bathroom. I need it anyway."

I throw my dress over me while Dovana scrambles for her pants. "You ready to finally find out?"

"Find out what?" I ask, wiping my mouth.

Her massive grin answers my question. Right, movies and pizza. "Damn, I'm good."

"You are," I breathe, staring up at her from my spot on the bed. "Is there anything I need to do? I'm just...I don't know what to expect. Pizza is food, right? And movies are...what?"

"You'll find out. But no, you're good just how you are. Just lie there with your hair all messed up. It's really working for you. I'll grab the pizza. We're dressed, by the way," she adds as she heads to the kitchen.

A minute later, she comes back with a cardboard box that smells like...is that bread? And tomatoes, maybe cheese? "What is that?"

She grabs something from the table between the beds and sets the box on my lap before climbing over my legs to sit next to me. "Sorry, I could've moved," I say.

"It's fine. I like being on you. All right, you ready? Open up the box."

I stare in awe at the second most beautiful thing I've seen today. "Wow." It's like bread, but it's covered in a bunch of things, sort of like a sandwich but without the top part. But the way the cheese is melted, and the almost taunting scent of the bread adds up to something irresistible. I don't even try. I grab a slice and hope that you're supposed to eat it with your hands as I take a massive bite of the thicker end.

"You're eating it backward," she mutters, grabbing her own piece. "You like it?"

I nod and flip it around, trying another bite. "It's perfection." It seems to almost melt in my mouth while this combination of flavors explodes. There're mushrooms and peppers on it that add an extra touch whenever I reach them, but the pizza itself is already even greater than sandwiches. Well, about as great. "Why have I been deprived of these things all my life? People leave out offerings for us, and I've visited a few families. Why was there never anything like this?"

She shrugs and wraps an arm around me. "I don't know, babe, but I'll make sure not to deprive you. Now, for your other question." She presses something on the object in her other hand, and the box in front of us lights up. "Shit, I forgot to put in the movie. Caroline?" she calls.

"Give me a minute," her voice answers from the bathroom.

"Would you put in *The Princess Bride*? We're doing this right."

"Yes," she shouts, sounding almost as excited as I must've while describing the pizza.

Caroline comes running down the short hallway-kitchen and grabs something from a bookcase. "All right. You sure you want to set her expectations this high? If this is her first movie, then all of the ones are going to seem disappointing."

"I think she'll manage."

I look between the two of them.

"All right. Let's do this." She pulls a disk out of the case and puts it in something else, then grabs a piece of pizza and takes a seat on the opposite bed.

"What the fuck?" I ask, jumping back in the bed and barely managing to stop the pizza from flying off. Images are flashing on the box, along with some very loud sounds.

Dovana's head smacks against the wall as she doubles over laughing. "Oh my fucking God. That was so worth it."

"What?" I ask. "How? What?"

"Okay. That was pretty great."

"I'm sorry," Dovana says. "I really don't know how to better explain it. Now just enjoy your food and watch the movie."

"But…what?"

"I know. I promise, it'll make sense soon."

It doesn't, but it's still interesting. I suppose it's sort of like a play but electronic. I feel like she could've just said that. Do humans still have plays?

We devour the entire pizza before the movie is even halfway through, but even without that ambrosia, it's still an entertaining experience, and I can hardly complain so long as I'm in her arms. Yeah, I think I'm going to get used to this.

Epilogue

The dean calls her name. "Dovana Gudaitiene." I finally get to see my wife graduate. Again. Hey, even the second graduation is pretty special. Though it would be a bit nicer if I didn't have to wear these stupid sunglasses, but apparently, people start shouting cyclops and running away if I don't, and I don't want to ruin her special day. Her mother sits on my left with her father beside her, and Matis sits on my other side. I swear, he's been obsessed with me ever since he found out I was real. He's even stopped fighting with Dovana. Mostly. Well, somewhat.

Dovana rushes onto the stage. I think she was talking to the girl behind her. Fiona's last name is right after hers, so I knew that would happen. She grins at us before shaking the dean's hand and taking her law school diploma. Ever since she realized how much people like me have trouble getting legal advice, she's completely thrown herself into her studies. She even made the dean's list most years.

I lean forward and turn my head, attempting to see the stage. My mother-in-law pats my shoulder, and I look at her, barely able to see her comforting smile. I suppose hearing it is enough. Dovana's still following her dreams and doing it all to help monsters…er, fiends as they're called here. Even Grandmother is proud.

Dovana leaves the stage, and her mother sits back, grinning over at me. "I'm proud of her too," she says.

"She really did it."

She nods, beaming. She used to be so worried that I was going to just let Dovana be all rich and comfortable since I can make gold. I've never seen anyone as excited as she was when she saw how invested Dovana was in becoming a lawyer. It's weird having the whole family agree. And get-togethers are still a bit much. But at least Mother and Matis seem to get along. She's already started spoiling him and adding to his college savings.

We whisper to each other about nothing in particular as we wait for the rest of the ceremony to finish. Chuckling, she says, "I'm so glad I don't teach at this school, or I'd actually be in some trouble here. When they're your students, graduation still isn't fun, but at least you're more invested. I really only know a handful of these kids."

"Hey," Dovana calls, waving as she runs over. She throws her arms around me, and I hug her back. I hadn't even known I'd missed her, but having her back in my arms makes me feel complete. How could I have ever considered resisting this? I love her.

She hugs her mother next. "I'm glad you came, Mama. I know you had class this morning. You can stay with us tonight if you want."

"The drive up to Montreal really wasn't that bad. Though, yes, we would love to stay the night. Maybe even the weekend if you'll have us."

She nods, grinning as she hugs her again. "Yes. Of course. You're always more than welcome. Right, babe?"

"Of course. Our home is your home."

"Not that it'll be your home for much longer," her father says. "You are still selling it, right?"

"Probably not for another year or two," I say.

Dovana adds, "Yeah, I need to get some experience first, and there's a firm in town that's already offered me a position. Then I can head back to Toronto and finally check out the new Community Center. God, we've never been so lucky as when the Honeydale Mall closed down."

"I still think they should've used Honest Eds," he mutters. "It's so big."

"You just wanted to see if they left anything behind." His wife elbows him playfully. "That sounds perfect. I suppose we'll have to find a way to handle the next few years with you all the way up here."

Matis says, "You can always come visit. There's still the woods by our house."

"I know. And we visit almost every week," Dovana says.

He stares at me.

"You know we'll keep visiting. And I'll try to bring you more from Lithuania next time. Anything in particular you want?"

He shakes his head. "I don't know. Whatever you think."

"Devynerios," Dovana whispers.

"Not for him," her mother shouts.

"I can drink it," he grumbles.

Their father ruffles his hair. "Two more years."

Matis crosses his arms and glares at them. "You wouldn't care if this was Lithuania."

"Of course we would," their mother says unconvincingly.

"Let's go get pizza," I suggest. I'm really trying not to sound too excited. It's been years by now. I'm used to it. It's not that special. But still, it's pizza!

"This is my celebration," Dovana says, chuckling and cutting it off by kissing me. "But I wanted to go to that Italian place anyway. And they have pizza."

I work to contain my joy. "Okay. If that's what you want, dearest."

The line is long, but we manage to make it back to the car and to the restaurant across town in just under an hour. We'd hoped that it wouldn't be crowded, but a few other graduates arrive around when we do, and there's already a small line at the door.

It's only three hours after her graduation when we finally get to eat.

But the dinner is wonderful. I don't think I've ever had pizza this good. Plus, we're celebrating Dovana's big life change and upcoming lawyer job and all of that exciting stuff. But also, it's bread with stuff on it, and it's amazing.

Dovana squeezes my hand, drawing my attention away from the delicacy. I don't even give it a lingering gaze. I'm absolutely mad for her. I knew it would happen, but I had no idea it would be this intense. I hold her hand to me, and she leans in, resting her head on my shoulder. It's been a long day, and I know she's exhausted. I can feel that slight call to look after her. It's strange, I had never known anything like that, but it gives me a piece of her even when we're apart.

I hold her closer, and for the first time in my life, I have no idea what's awaiting us. I never saw beyond this, and so far, our life together is a far better fate than I could have foreseen, and I can't wait to see what's to come.

About the Author

Genevieve McCluer was born in California and grew up in numerous cities across the country. She studied criminal justice in college but, after a few years of that, moved her focus to writing. Her whole life, she's been obsessed with mythology, and she bases her stories in those myths.

She now lives in Arizona with her partner and cats, working away at far too many novels. In her free time she pesters the cats, plays video games, and attempts to be better at archery.

Books Available from Bold Strokes Books

A Fae Tale by Genevieve McCluer. Dovana comes to terms with her changing feelings for her lifelong best friend and fae, Roze. (978-1-63555-918-7)

Accidental Desperados by Lee Lynch. Life is clobbering Berry, Jaudon, and their long romance. The arrival of directionless baby dyke MJ doesn't help. Can they find their passion again—and keep it? (978-1-63555-482-3)

Always Believe by Aimée. Greyson Waldsen is pursuing ordination as an Anglican priest. Angela Arlingham doesn't believe in God. Do they follow their vocation or their hearts? (978-1-63555-912-5)

Best of the Wrong Reasons by Sander Santiago. For Fin Ness and Orion Starr, it takes a funeral to remind them that love is worth living for. (978-1-63555-867-8)

Courage by Jesse J. Thoma. No matter how often Natasha Parsons and Tommy Finch clash on the job, an undeniable attraction simmers just beneath the surface. Can they find the courage to change so love has room to grow? (978-1-63555-802-9)

I Am Chris by R Kent. There's one saving grace to losing everything and moving away. Nobody knows her as Chrissy Taylor. Now Chris can live who he truly is. (978-1-63555-904-0)

The Princess and the Odium by Sam Ledel. Jastyn and Princess Aurelia return to Venostes and join their families in a battle against the dark force to take back their homeland for a chance at a better tomorrow. (978-1-63555-894-4)

The Queen Has a Cold by Jane Kolven. What happens when the heir to the throne isn't a prince or a princess? (978-1-63555-878-4)

The Secret Poet by Georgia Beers. Agreeing to help her brother woo Zoe Blake seemed like a good idea to Morgan Thompson at first...until she realizes she's actually wooing Zoe for herself... (978-1-63555-858-6)

You Again by Aurora Rey. For high school sweethearts Kate Cormier and Sutton Guidry, the second chance might be the only one that matters. (978-1-63555-791-6)

Coming to Life on South High by Lee Patton. Twenty-one-year-old gay virgin Gabe Rafferty's first adult decade unfolds as an unpredictable journey into sex, love, and livelihood. (978-1-63555-906-4)

Fleur d'Lies by MJ Williamz. For rookie cop DJ Sander, being true to what you believe is the only way to live...and one way to die. (978-1-63555-854-8)

Love's Falling Star by B.D. Grayson. For country music megastar Lochlan Paige, can love conquer her fear of losing the one thing she's worked so hard to protect? (978-1-63555-873-9)

Love's Truth by C.A. Popovich. Can Lynette and Barb make love work when unhealed wounds of betrayed trust and a secret could change everything? (978-1-63555-755-8)

Next Exit Home by Dena Blake. Home may be where the heart is, but for Harper Sims and Addison Foster, is the journey back worth the pain? (978-1-63555-727-5)

Not Broken by Lyn Hemphill. Falling in love is hard enough—even more so for Rose who's carrying her ex's baby. (978-1-63555-869-2)

The Noble and the Nightingale by Barbara Ann Wright. Two women on opposite sides of empires at war risk all for a chance at love. (978-1-63555-812-8)

What a Tangled Web by Melissa Brayden. Clementine Monroe has the chance to buy the café she's managed for years, but Madison LeGrange swoops in and buys it first. Now Clementine is forced to work for the enemy and ignore her former crush. (978-1-63555-749-7)

A Far Better Thing by JD Wilburn. When needs of her family and wants of her heart clash, Cass Halliburton is faced with the ultimate sacrifice. (978-1-63555-834-0)

Body Language by Renee Roman. When Mika offers to provide Jen erotic tutoring, will sex drive them into a deeper relationship or tear them apart? (978-1-63555-800-5)

Carrie and Hope by Joy Argento. For Carrie and Hope loss brings them together but secrets and fear may tear them apart. (978-1-63555-827-2)

Death's Prelude by David S. Pederson. In this prequel to the Detective Heath Barrington Mystery series, Heath discovers that first love changes you forever and drives you to become the person you're destined to be. (978-1-63555-786-2)

Ice Queen by Gun Brooke. School counselor Aislin Kennedy wants to help standoffish CEO Susanna Durr and her troubled teenage daughter become closer—even if it means risking her own heart in the process. (978-1-63555-721-3)

Masquerade by Anne Shade. In 1925 Harlem, New York, a notorious gangster sets her sights on seducing Celine, and new lovers Dinah and Celine are forced to risk their hearts, and lives, for love. (978-1-63555-831-9)

Royal Family by Jenny Frame. Loss has defined both Clay's and Katya's lives, but guarding their hearts may prove to be the biggest heartbreak of all. (978-1-63555-745-9)

Share the Moon by Toni Logan. Three best friends, an inherited vineyard and a resident ghost come together for fun, romance and a touch of magic. (978-1-63555-844-9)

Spirit of the Law by Carsen Taite. Attorney Owen Lassiter will do almost anything to put a murderer behind bars, but can she get past her reluctance to rely on unconventional help from the alluring Summer Byrne and keep from falling in love in the process? (978-1-63555-766-4)

The Devil Incarnate by Ali Vali. Cain Casey has so much to live for, but enemies who lurk in the shadows threaten to unravel it all. (978-1-63555-534-9)

His Brother's Viscount by Stephanie Lake. Hector Somerville wants to rekindle his illicit love affair with Viscount Wentworth, but he must overcome one problem: Wentworth still loves Hector's brother. (978-1-63555-805-0)

Journey to Cash by Ashley Bartlett. Cash Braddock thought everything was great, but it looks like her history is about to become her right now. Which is a real bummer. (978-1-63555-464-9)

Liberty Bay by Karis Walsh. Wren Lindley's life is mired in tradition and untouched by trends until social media star Gina Strickland introduces an irresistible electricity into her off-the-grid world. (978-1-63555-816-6)

Scent by Kris Bryant. Nico Marshall has been burned by women in the past wanting her for her money. This time, she's determined to win Sophia Sweet over with her charm. (978-1-63555-780-0)

Shadows of Steel by Suzie Clarke. As their worlds collide and their choices come back to haunt them, Rachel and Claire must figure out how to stay together and most of all, stay alive. (978-1-63555-810-4)

The Clinch by Nicole Disney. Eden Bauer overcame a difficult past to become a world champion mixed martial artist, but now rising star and dreamy bad girl Brooklyn Shaw is a threat both to Eden's title and her heart. (978-1-63555-820-3)

The Last First Kiss by Julie Cannon. Kelly Newsome is so ready for a tropical island vacation, but she never expects to meet the woman who could give her her last first kiss. (978-1-63555-768-8)

The Mandolin Lunch by Missouri Vaun. Despite their immediate attraction, everything about Garet Allen says short-term, and Tess Hill refuses to consider anything less than forever. (978-1-63555-566-0)

Thor: Daughter of Asgard by Genevieve McCluer. When Hannah Olsen finds out she's the reincarnation of Thor, she's thrown into a world of magic and intrigue, unexpected attraction, and a mystery she's got to unravel. (978-1-63555-814-2)

Veterinary Technician by Nancy Wheelton. When a stable of horses is threatened Val and Ronnie must work together against the odds to save them, and maybe even themselves along the way. (978-1-63555-839-5)

16 Steps to Forever by Georgia Beers. Can Brooke Sullivan and Macy Carr find themselves by finding each other? (978-1-63555-762-6)

All I Want for Christmas by Georgia Beers, Maggie Cummings, Fiona Riley. The Christmas season sparks passion and love in these stories by award winning authors Georgia Beers, Maggie Cummings, and Fiona Riley. (978-1-63555-764-0)

From the Woods by Charlotte Greene. When Fiona goes backpacking in a protected wilderness, the last thing she expects is to be fighting for her life. (978-1-63555-793-0)

Heart of the Storm by Nicole Stiling. For Juliet Mitchell and Sienna Bennett a forbidden attraction definitely isn't worth upending the life they've worked so hard for. Is it? (978-1-63555-789-3)

If You Dare by Sandy Lowe. For Lauren West and Emma Prescott, following their passions is easy. Following their hearts, though? That's almost impossible. (978-1-63555-654-4)

Love Changes Everything by Jaime Maddox. For Samantha Brooks and Kirby Fielding, no matter how careful their plans, love will change everything. (978-1-63555-835-7)

Not This Time by MA Binfield. Flung back into each other's lives, can former bandmates Sophia and Madison have a second chance at romance? (978-1-63555-798-5)

The Dubious Gift of Dragon Blood by J. Marshall Freeman. One day Crispin is a lonely high school student—the next he is fighting a war in a land ruled by dragons, his otherworldly boyfriend at his side. (978-1-63555-725-1)

The Found Jar by Jaycie Morrison. Fear keeps Emily Harris trapped in her emotionally vacant life; can she find the courage to let Beck Reynolds guide her toward love? (978-1-63555-825-8)